SNOW AND MISTLETOE IN EDEN FALLS

A CLEAN, OPPOSITES ATTRACT ROMANCE

TINA NEWCOMB

To Booklovers

Noun: Someone who loves (and usually collects) books

CHAPTER 1

"Hello?"

When he heard the female voice, Kevin Klein checked his cell phone screen. The number was definitely his brother's. *Nice greeting—way to go, bro.* "Is Ethan there?"

"Nope. Sorry, you must have the wrong number." *Click.*

After the call disconnected, Kevin scrolled through his contacts and was careful to press Ethan's number.

"Did you think if you called right back the number would magically be Ethan's?" asked the same female with a laugh.

"This has been Ethan's cell number since he got his first phone at fourteen."

"Well, he must have changed his number. Have a good day." *Click.*

She'd hung up on him for the second time. Out of frustration, he hit the number again.

"Look, I don't have time to play this little game with you. Today's the first day of a new job and I won't be able to leave on time if you keep calling."

"Ethan would have told me if he changed his number."

"Maybe you don't know this Ethan as well as you think you do."

"I've known my brother since the day he was born, so yeah, I know him pretty well."

"I don't know what to tell you except to repeat that this is my number and there is no Ethan here, so goodbye."

"Wait! At least tell me how long you've had this number."

He heard her irritable sigh loud and clear. "About three weeks."

Had it been that long since he called Ethan? Kevin checked the Klein's Auto Shop calendar on the reception area wall—it was now the first week of December. He'd talked to Ethan on Thanksgiving when Mom called him on her landline and they just passed the receiver around. He ran his fingers through his hair. Maybe it *had* been three weeks since he called his brother.

"Hello-o-o?" the female singsonged. Even irritable she had a sexy voice, sweet with a touch of rust. "I'm hanging up."

"Yeah. Sorry to bother you."

Kevin stuffed his phone into his back pocket and walked out of the office and into the garage bay. The acrid smell of motor oil, the tangy scent of metal, and the pungent odor of rubber surrounded him in a cocoon of familiarity. Nate, brother number three of five, had his head under the hood of brother number two's 1970s Camaro. The car was a beauty, and Max's pride and joy. Max sat on a nearby workbench, staring intensely at Nate's back. Though two years apart, his brothers looked like they could be twins. Except for Max's scowl. None of them could quite match Max's furrow-browed frown.

Nate straightened and tugged a greasy rag out of the back pocket of his overalls and turned to Max. "Sounds fine to me."

Max threw up his arms. "Come on, bro. How can you not hear that pinging sound?"

"Maybe a worn water pump bearing," Nate said with a shake of his head.

"I know what a worn water pump bearing sounds like. This is different. It's a high-pitched ping."

"Maybe you need your hearing checked," Kevin said as he approached them. "Did either of you knuckleheads know Ethan changed his number?"

Max jumped off the workbench, opened the driver's door, and switched off the engine. "Sounds like the only knuckle-head around here is you for not knowing. And Nate for not being able to hear."

Good-natured Nate ignored the remark with a shrug.

"Why would he change numbers?"

"That psycho ex-girlfriend wouldn't stop harassing him," Max said.

Kevin picked a candy wrapper up off the garage floor and held it out for Max. His brother—nicknamed the slob—had a bad habit of leaving his trash wherever it dropped. "You mean the girl who wasn't a girlfriend but thought she was?"

"Yep," Max answered, wadding up the wrapper and aiming for the trash can. "He jumps! He shoots!"

The paper hit the rim and bounced off, rolling under the Camaro, where it would stay until Kevin or Nate picked it up again. Kevin leveled a look at his brother.

"What? You can't sink 'em all."

"You never sink any," Nate said.

"Okay, what's Ethan's new number?" Kevin asked.

Nate pointed to his phone, which was sitting on the workbench. "Check my contacts. I think I have the right number."

Kevin found Ethan's name, entered the new number, and tried again. This time he got Ethan's voice mail.

"Hey, bro, thanks for the heads-up about changing your number. For Christmas we're all pitching in to give Mom and Murray a trip to Victoria Island. Give me a call when you have a minute so I can fill you in on the details."

"Glad you reminded me," Max said after Kevin disconnected the call. He pulled out his wallet and handed over some bills.

"Jolie wrote you a check this morning. I left it sitting on the desk in the office," Nate said, opening the hood of a white Toyota.

Money was tighter for Nate than for the rest of the brothers. He'd married his high school sweetheart three years ago and bought a new house. His wife, Jolie, hadn't gone back to work since their darling baby girl—who had the entire family wrapped around her sweet little finger—was born.

Kevin hated the hint of jealousy he felt because a younger brother had found love and was settled and had started his own family, while love was elusive as Bigfoot for him.

Sure, Kevin had a nice life and a booming business, but he had no one to share it with. Most of his friends were married, owned homes, and had kids. Going home every night to the apartment he shared with Max was getting harder and harder. He felt discontented, antsy for more.

Kevin nodded toward the Toyota. "When did that one come in?"

"It was parked out front. A lady left a message on the answering machine, said the engine has been overheating," Nate said. "She put her keys in the drop box."

Kevin knew most everyone in town and knew what they drove, but the Toyota wasn't familiar to him. "She didn't leave a name?"

The bell in the reception area echoed through the bay before Nate could answer.

"Time to move your car out, Max. We have customers."

Kevin opened the bay door behind Max's car so he could back out.

Inside the office, postal worker Rita Reynolds peeled off gloves and unwound a scarf three times the length of her body from around her neck. The woman never made an appointment. Just dropped off her car and expected them to put it at the top of their list of repairs.

"Hey, Rita," Kevin said. "What can we do for you today?"

Squawk! She flapped her arms—one of her many birdlike habits—as if she might take flight any minute. "Don't give me any grief, Kevin Klein. I told Nate I needed an oil change and he said I could come in anytime."

"I wasn't going to give you grief." *Like that would do any good.* "We can get to it this morning."

"Okay, well, come on then." She started to rewind the scarf.

"Where are we going?"

"I need a ride to work!" She flapped a hand toward the window. "You don't expect me to walk to the post office in this blizzard, do you?"

"Blizzard" was a bit of an exaggeration, but the snow was coming down steadily. He hit the intercom button on the wall. "Max, bring Rita's car in next for an oil change. I'm going to run her over to the post office. Be right back." Both Max and Nate waved without looking his way. He grabbed his coat from the rack and held the door open for Rita. The tiny woman glared up at him as she passed.

Normally he'd take his truck, especially with the snowy roads, because the bed was loaded with bags of sand. But Rita couldn't climb up into the passenger seat, and he wasn't about to lift her. He led her to a Subaru. If he'd trusted her driving, he'd have just let her take the car as a loaner, but Rita was forever getting tickets for her fast, reckless driving around town.

He unlocked the passenger door and waited until she slid into place before running around to start the car. He'd scrape the windows while the engine warmed up.

She glared at him through her thick-lensed glasses, her eyes magnified to scary proportions. *Squawk!* "You hurry up now, Kevin, or I'll be late."

The second woman of the morning blaming him because *she* was going to be late. "Yes, ma'am." He turned the heat to high, grabbed the scraper, and shut the door. Once the windows were clear, he climbed in and drove Rita around Town Square with her complaining the whole way. When they reached the post office, he pulled into the special drive-thru lane lined with mailboxes.

Squawk! "You're not supposed to park here. This is for letter drop-off only."

"I'm not parking. Just trying to get you close to the door, Rita."

"Driving through here without a letter is in direct violation of post office policies."

"I won't ever do it again." He leaned across the console and opened her door. "Out you go. We'll call when your car is ready."

"I'll need someone to pick me up."

"Yep. Got it. One of us will come and get you." *But it won't be me.* He unclipped her seat belt. "Bye, Rita. Have a great day."

She took two full minutes to climb out of his car, pull her hat lower over her ears, adjust her coat, and sling her purse over her head. The car behind him honked. Bending down, she shook a gloved finger at him. "See, I told you this drive-thru is for mailing letters only. You have three cars lined up behind you. You may just get a ticket for this stunt, Kevin Klein."

They're not waiting for me. They're waiting for you! "Okay,

Rita. If you'll shut the door, I can get out of their way." *And she's flapping her arms again.*

"This sidewalk is slippery."

Kevin jumped out, held up a hand to let the cars behind him know he was sorry, and rounded the car. He took Rita's arm to steady her and shut the door. The car behind him honked again.

He looked skyward. *Please, help me get through this morning.*

"You don't have to manhandle me."

"I'm not manhandling. I'm holding your arm to keep you from slipping."

"I'm going to have bruises from your rough treatment."

"Pretty sure I'm not holding your arm tight enough to give you bruises." He got her up on the curb and walked her to the post office's front door. "There you go."

A woman coming down the sidewalk stopped next to Rita. "Are you okay? Is he hurting you?" she asked, her voice muffled by the scarf wrapped around the lower half of her face.

"He's manhandling me."

Kevin threw up his hands in surrender. "I'm not manhandling you, Rita." He glanced at the woman. Everything was covered but a pair of the bluest eyes he'd ever seen. "I was helping her to the door so she wouldn't slip."

Blue-eyes glanced from him to Rita and back, then pointed to his car. "You do know that's a drive-thru lane for dropping off letters. It's not a parking lot."

"Got it," he said over his shoulder as he jogged to the Subaru. "Sorry to ruin everyone's day while I helped an old lady to the door."

Squawk! "Who are you calling an old lady?"

"Sorry, Rita." He climbed behind the wheel and pulled onto the street before he glanced in the rearview mirror. Rita and the woman stood where he'd left them, both glaring in his direction. "Happy Monday," he muttered.

~

*R*onnie Coleman walked past the sign that said *Owen Danielson, Attorney-at-Law,* and up the steps to the porch of the beautiful Victorian.

She wasn't sure why she was so nervous about reporting for her first day of work. Maybe because of the move to a new town and her frustrating morning.

Her interview with Owen had gone well. The guy was a little geeky, but extremely nice, with a calming aura she really liked. He was the kind of man who would put his clients at immediate ease. The last attorney she'd worked for was demanding, high-strung, disorganized, and quick to blame others for his mistakes. She'd gotten tired of making excuses to his clients and covering for him with other attorneys.

When she got wind of this job, she'd sent her resume and Owen called the next day to set up an interview. She'd happily driven the three hours from Spokane to Eden Falls. A week later, Owen offered her the job, and she returned to the quaint little town to find a place to live.

Ronnie stomped the snow off her boots and entered the beautiful foyer that served as the reception area of the home-turned-office. She loved that Owen had built his business in the restored Victorian. He said his wife tried to keep the décor true to the era of the home, and Ronnie loved the rich, soothing, earthy colors she'd used. Smart choices since most people were nervous when they first walked through the door of an attorney's office.

The Christmas tree at the front window was lit against the dark of the day, and garlands were strung around doorways. A wreath hung over a blazing fire, which lent both warmth and a rich glow to the room.

Owen came down the hall with a hospitable smile. "Welcome to Eden Falls and the office. Did you get moved into your new place?"

"I did. Thanks for the recommendation." Mrs. O'Malley's basement apartment was small but doable. Being single and petless, Ronnie didn't need much space. Mrs. O'Malley had said that the woman who lived there before had painted the dark wood paneling white, which brightened the underground apartment.

"How was your Thanksgiving?"

She pulled off her hat and gloves. "It was nice. Yours?"

"Very good." Owen rocked back on his heels. "We went back east to celebrate with my in-laws. My schedule doesn't allow us to visit often."

"Thanks for letting me start after the holiday weekend," Ronnie said, shrugging out of her coat and hanging her things on a beautiful iron coat stand by the door.

He waved her thanks away. "We all like to spend holidays with those we love."

Thanksgiving had been tense at her parents' house since they weren't happy about her move to Eden Falls. Other than college, she'd never lived anywhere but Spokane. As an only child with loving but extremely overprotective parents, she'd felt an urgency to spread her wings—although *escape* might be closer to the truth. "Sorry I'm a little late. I had car trouble."

"Oh, no!" he said with genuine kindness. "I'm sorry to hear that. We have a great auto shop on—"

"Klein's?"

Owen nodded, adjusting his glasses. "That's the one."

"I dropped my car off early this morning."

"The Klein brothers are the best around. Honest and reliable."

She set her purse on what would be her desk. "I hope they're also fast. It's a little too cold to be carless."

"They're fast. If it's not ready by four I'll give you a ride. You can't go wrong with Klein's." He turned and beckoned her to follow him down the hall. "We have coffee, tea, and hot cocoa in the kitchen. Let's get something warm in you, then we'll get started."

Ronnie followed, appreciating Owen's jaunty step, deciding right away that she was going to like working for him.

CHAPTER 2

Kevin parked Rita's car behind the post office and took her keys inside. Thankfully she had too many customers mailing packages and buying Christmas stamps to question him about every little thing they'd done to the car.

"Hey, Kevin." Dawson Garrett motioned for him to come behind the counter where he was sorting packages. Dawson had been the postmaster of Eden Falls for as long as Kevin could remember. "I have a delivery for your mom. Will you be seeing her tonight?"

"Sure. I can drop it by."

"How're she and Murray doing?"

"Good." Kevin set Rita's bill and keys on the table near Dawson, and wedged the package under his arm. "Mom's busy with the church bazaar."

"Oh, that's right. She was brave enough to volunteer to chair this year. Tell her to call us if she needs anything. Alice is free most days, at least until our new grandson is born, and I can help in the evenings."

"When is Alex due?"

"About two weeks."

Kevin patted him on the shoulder. "Congrats, and I'll pass the word on to Mom." He pointed toward the keys. "Tell Rita her car is parked out back. She can call if she has any problems."

Dawson laughed. "Oh, you can count on that. She'll call even if she doesn't have a problem."

"You got that right. See you around, Dawson."

Outside the snow was still coming down, but not quite as hard. Tucking the package under his coat, he tugged on his knit beanie and gloves. Eden Falls was a winter wonderland, the streets hushed with snow, as he walked the few blocks back to the shop.

A sense of pride swept over him every time the Klein's Auto Shop sign came into view. Nate, Max, and he had been repairing engines in their mom and stepdad's garage since high school. After graduation, he took some business classes at the community college, and a couple of years later their stepdad loaned them the money to build their own garage.

Since they were the only repair shop in town, their business grew quickly. Because they offered fair prices and were good at what they did, word of mouth spread their excellent reputation beyond Eden Falls' town limits. With a solid business plan and their first-rate reputation, they were able to repay their stepfather a year ahead of time. Out of the five Klein brothers, only Ethan and Cameron—the two youngest —decided on different career paths.

He often wondered where they would be if his mom hadn't met Murray Pierce. Murray moved them from a two-bedroom apartment, where his mom slept on the sofa, to a farmhouse on the outskirts of town. He made it possible for his mom to quit her second job and then become a stay-at-home mom. He raised her boys as his own, paid off old debts, made sure they all had clothes that fit and shoes without holes. Murray was more of a father than their deadbeat dad had ever been.

None of them had any trouble accepting Murray into their lives. He made their mother happy, and she deserved some happiness after being left with five little boys to raise on her own.

He entered the garage by the side door. Max had his car in the bay, again listening for the nonexistent ping, and Nate was at the sink scrubbing his hands.

"What was wrong with that Toyota this morning?"

"Just a hose," Nate replied.

Max straightened. "Come listen to this engine, Kevin."

"There is no pinging sound, Max. You've got a great car. Take it for a drive and enjoy it before there really is a problem." Kevin headed for the office. "I've got to deliver this package to Mom. I'll see you two later."

~

After work, Ronnie hitched a ride to Klein's Auto Shop with Owen. A guy named Nate had called around lunchtime to tell her they'd found the problem, a radiator hose. When he quoted the price, she was pleasantly surprised. What with starting a new job, the move, and Christmas around the corner, she didn't have a lot of cash to spare for car repairs.

Inside, the reception area was cozy warm and freakishly clean. Another surprise. A cute guy stood behind the counter. He looked up from a magazine he was thumbing through and grinned.

"How can I help you?"

She peeled off her gloves. "Are you Nate?"

The guy shook his head and pointed to a wall of windows

showcasing a brightly lit garage. "Nate's under the hood of a Ford."

"He called to say my car's ready. A white Toyota."

"Ah, the radiator hose. Wish all problems were that easy to fix."

She pulled her wallet out of her purse. "I wish all problems were that cheap."

"Wouldn't that be nice?" The guy had a great smile and expressive eyes that hinted at a bit of playfulness. "Are you new in town?"

"Just moved in over the weekend."

He slipped her credit card into the machine. "What brings you to Eden Falls?"

"A job."

The guy's smile grew. "Yeah? Where?"

"I started working for an attorney."

"Must be Owen Danielson, since he's the only attorney in town. My sister-in-law"—he hitched his thumb toward the garage bay—"Nate's wife, Jolie, used to work for Owen."

"Really?" The connection to her new boss piqued her curiosity. "Do you know why she quit? If you don't mind me asking," she added quickly.

"She decided to stay at home after my niece was born."

Good to know her reason wasn't because she hated the job or despised working for Owen, who was really an ogre in sheep's clothing.

"Jolie loved her job. I'm sure she'd be happy to talk to you if you have any questions."

"If I run into problems, I'll get her number."

The guy handed over the Toyota keys and her receipt. "You're all set. Your car is parked on the side."

"I appreciate how quickly you were able to get the problem fixed. The weather makes walking inconvenient, even in this small town."

"Winter came early this year." They both glanced toward the front window. Snow was falling again. "Welcome to Eden Falls."

"Thank you." She stuffed the receipt into her bag and wiggled her fingers into her gloves.

Outside, the snow was blowing sideways. Going to the grocery store in this weather wasn't something she relished. Luckily her mom had loaded several boxes of groceries into the moving van before Ronnie left Spokane.

All the shops around Town Square were lit against the wintery day. Brightly colored lights hung from a huge pine in the center of the square and decorated most windows, while swags of greenery spruced up the old-fashioned light posts. If the wind wasn't hurricane-force, the scene would be picturesque.

Still, Eden Falls was charming, and she could hardly wait to explore the shops, especially the pastry shop.

Darkness had fallen by the time she reached Mrs. O'Malley's house. Quickly changing from her knit dress and heeled boots to warm pants and winter boots, she headed back outdoors. As part of her rental contract, she'd agreed to shovel the driveway and front walk, something she certainly didn't mind doing since the rent her landlord charged was ridiculously low. Starting at the front porch, she worked her way down the driveway, along the sidewalk, then around the house to her basement apartment. The job took her a long, chilly hour.

Cold and hungry by the time she was back in her apartment, she wished she had a fireplace to warm her up. Instead she settled for a bowl of soup. Then, tucking her feet under her, she cozied up on the sofa with a blanket, a cup of hot cocoa, and a book she hoped was as good as the reviews indicated. Before she opened the cover, her cell phone rang. She recognized the number lighting the screen as the one belonging to the guy who'd repeatedly called this morning.

"Hello?"

"Hi," he said after a pregnant pause.

She heard the smile in his voice. "Did you ever find Ethan?"

A husky chuckle followed her question. "I did. According to my brothers, he changed his number when his psycho girlfriend—who technically wasn't ever a girlfriend—wouldn't leave him alone."

"Ahh, everything begins to make sense," Ronnie said. "I think that girlfriend called me a couple of times, though she never used Ethan's name. Just wanted to know who I was and why I was answering her boyfriend's phone. I guess I finally convinced her the guy had changed his number."

"Sorry I kept calling this morning. Hope you weren't late for work."

Ronnie set her book aside. "Only a few minutes. I'm lucky to have a new boss who didn't mind."

"How was your first day?"

"A few bumps in the road, but for the most part I had a good day."

"Mind if I ask what you do?"

Ronnie tucked a throw pillow under her arm and ran fingertips against the nap, standing the soft velvet on end. "I'm a glorified secretary. My official title is executive assistant. I'm hoping that changes soon."

"I don't know, 'executive assistant' sounds pretty official." The guy laughed. She liked the sound of his deep voice. "Mind if I ask what you do?" she said, repeating his question.

"I'm a mechanic. My official title is auto technician."

This time she laughed. "No way. I could have used you today." Maybe she shouldn't have said that. Though why not? She didn't know this man. The area code at the front of his number covered three-fourths of the state of Washington. And with the freedom of cell phones, he could live in another state. Heck, he could live anywhere.

"Uh-oh, car trouble?"

"Yes, but the problem was minor."

"Good to hear. Car repairs can get expensive."

"Another bit of luck, I have a great auto shop close by." She hoped he didn't ask where she lived. The anonymity was better. Safer. She didn't have a great track record with men, and she certainly wouldn't give that information out to a stranger.

A long pause followed, where she searched for something to say. Her apartment felt a little less lonely while she was talking to this man with the nice laugh. Then again, for all she knew, he could be a crazy serial killer or as psychotic as his brother's ex-not-girlfriend. "Is it cold where you are?"

"Yes. Cold and snowing. How about you?" He could live next door by the description he'd just given.

"Tonight's bitter," she said. "I had to shovel the driveway and sidewalk when I got home, and now I can't seem to get warm."

"You must live in a house."

She laughed. "The basement of a house."

"I'm jealous. I share an apartment with my brother."

At times talking to someone you didn't know could be easier than sitting face-to-face with someone you'd known forever. Like her parents. Or her last boyfriend. They had tried to make their relationship work despite having very little in common. The popular saying "opposites attract" might be true, but if there was nothing to hold those opposites together, all the attraction in the world meant zilch. "Nothing to be jealous of. My basement apartment is pretty small."

"Do you share the space with someone?"

His way of asking if I live with a boyfriend? Or husband? "Nope. Just me. I don't even have a pet goldfish."

"Our apartment doesn't allow pets," he said.

Another pause fell over their conversation. They'd covered careers and living arrangements. What else did strangers talk about? "You said you live with your brother. Do you have a lot of family close by?"

"Two brothers, and my mom and stepdad, live close."

"No sisters?"

"No sisters. Do you have siblings?"

Another stab of loneliness hit her. "No. Again, just me."

"Again, I'm jealous."

"No you're not. I would have loved to have a brother or sister or both. One of each. Any combination."

He laughed, and she wondered if his eyes lit up or crinkled much at the corners. Was he a happy person, or did he just sound that way over the phone? Did he have a dimple? She loved dimples.

"You say that now," he said.

She heard a door shut on his end of the call. Brother or girlfriend? Though he'd asked if she lived with someone, they really hadn't covered the boyfriend-girlfriend situation.

"I should let you go. Glad your first day only had minor problems."

"Glad you found Ethan. I guess you can forget my number now."

"I've been calling this number for ten years. Not sure I can stop that easily."

Good. She wouldn't mind hearing from him again.

~

*A*fter her goodbye, Kevin disconnected the call.

"What are you smiling about?" Max asked, walking into the kitchen.

What *was* he smiling about? He and the captivating voice hadn't shared much, hadn't exchanged so much as names, but Kevin had never felt so comfortable talking to a woman. And they hadn't even talked for long, just for a few minutes, sharing inane details of their day, revealing few secrets. He knew she worked as a secretary or assistant, today was her first day at a new job, and her car was giving her trouble. Just because her area code was the same as his didn't give much of a clue about where she lived.

He held his phone up. "Wrong number with a sexy voice."

"The best kind of wrong number." Max opened the fridge. "Want to go to Noelle's for dinner?"

"Too cold out." Kevin nudged Max out of the way. "Mom gave me some beef stew and a loaf of fresh bread when I dropped that package off."

"Enough for me?"

"No." He punched Max's shoulder. "Do you really think *our* mom wouldn't send enough for both of us?"

Max sliced the bread while Kevin heated the stew. His thoughts cycled back to the mysterious woman, trying to picture what she might look like by the sound of her voice, which was impossible, of course.

Kevin dished up the stew. "Grab the milk and a couple of glasses."

"The owner of the white Toyota came in after you left, said she was new in town," Max said, placing the milk and bread on the table.

"She?"

Max dipped a slice of bread in his stew. "Yep, and I call dibs."

Kevin laughed. "You call dibs? What are you, twelve?"

"Nope, I'm all grown up, but I know you."

"What does that mean?" Kevin asked, sitting at the table.

"Because you're *the big brother*," Max used air quotes, "you think you get first choice."

"You're an idiot. I've never thought that." Besides, he had a mystery voice to follow up on.

"Her name is Veronica. Kind of an old-fashioned name, but she has the prettiest blue eyes."

Kevin glanced up from his dinner, remembering the blue-eyed stranger who'd come to Rita's rescue this morning. "I might have run into her when I dropped Rita off at the post office." He chuckled. "Like you said, you called dibs. I wish you luck."

CHAPTER 3

*R*onnie grabbed her ringing phone and held her breath a moment while hitting *Decline Call*. She'd actually saved the number lighting her screen under *Mystery Man* with a picture of a handsome stranger. She hadn't heard from him in two days and, unfortunately, she couldn't talk now. Scrolling through her contacts, she hit the message icon below his name.

Sorry, can't talk.

Busy at work?

Yes

Talk later?

She paused, her thumb hesitating over Y. What was she doing? She didn't know this guy, didn't know anything about him. Maybe that was the perfect reason to be doing this. Anonymous, friendly flirting. No harm, no foul. No meeting up. Just a little talking, texting back and forth. Nobody gets hurt.

Yes

Turning to the copy machine, she sorted the stack of papers Owen needed for this afternoon.

Working for him was like falling into the supreme job, that once-in-a-lifetime opportunity that was set aside for the perfect person, and you were that perfect person. For the first time since she graduated from college, she was using her paralegal degree rather than doing legal work for a secretary's wages. Owen was a generous employer, and she felt lucky to have this break at a time when she needed a change.

She loved living out of her parents' reach. The three-hour drive kept them from popping in unexpectedly, so for the first time in her life, she was totally on her own. They'd followed her to Eden Falls—just to make sure she arrived safely. After helping her get everything inside her apartment and meeting her incredible landlady, they'd wanted to stay and help her settle in, but she rushed them out. She'd wanted to set up her living space on her own. She'd go home for a day or two over the Christmas holidays, and she'd invite them to visit. Someday. Soon. Maybe.

She heard the front door open and hurried out to the reception area to meet Owen's next client. The woman standing by the door pulling a knit cap off a dark-haired baby was not Mr. Polanski.

"Hi. Can I help you?"

The woman smiled as she rocked the baby back and forth. "Actually, I was wondering if I could help you. I'm Jolie Klein."

The name was familiar, but Ronnie couldn't make the connection.

"I used to work for Owen."

"Oh, right. Nate's wife."

The woman raised her eyebrows. "You know my husband?"

Ronnie set the stack of papers on the reception desk. "Not exactly. My car was overheating and I left it at his shop. I've only talked to him on the phone." She stepped forward and shook Jolie's hand. "Anyway, it's very nice to meet you. I'm Ronnie Coleman."

"Jolie," Owen said, coming down the hall. "I thought I heard your voice." He reached out and the baby fell into his arms as if he snuggled with her every day. "Hello, sweet Riley. You grow more beautiful every time I see you." The little girl giggled and patted his cheek. "Is she walking?"

"As long as she's holding onto something. She doesn't dare let go yet." Jolie dropped the baby's diaper bag on a chair.

"How old is she?" Ronnie asked. She didn't know anything about babies, had never even held one. This tiny girl looked too small to walk or even sit up alone.

"She'll be ten months next week."

When the baby turned her four-tooth grin on Ronnie, her heart hitched in a way she'd never experienced. Funny how powerful a smile could be. "She's adorable."

"Thank you. She's fun, but can make life . . . interesting at times."

"If you'll excuse me, I have more copies to make. It was nice to meet you, Jolie." Ronnie turned back to the copy room—which, if she guessed right, used to be a butler's pantry in the Victorian—leaving Owen and Jolie to talk. She caught bits and pieces of their hushed conversation from down the hall.

"How's she doing?"

"Very well."

"I bet it's nice to finally have a paralegal."

"I won't lie. She's been a big help already."

"That's great, Owen. I'm glad she's working out for you. I was worried about leaving."

"I'm going to hire a receptionist after the New Year so Ronnie can focus on other things. My office seems to get busier by the day."

Ronnie felt evil for listening in, so she shut the door. Owen's comment about hiring a receptionist to free her up for other things inspired a boost of confidence. He was just as generous with compliments as he was with her salary. Her last work environment had been so different. The lawyer drove his team for long hours. Morale was low and the employee turnover rate at the office high, but no amount of reasoning with the guy did any good. If he lost a case, it was the team members' fault. And if he won, he accepted all the credit without so much as a thanks.

Life at home had been fairly similar. Not that her parents expected perfection, though her mom and dad did set the bar high. Because she was their only child, she didn't want to let them or herself down.

Someone knocked lightly before the door opened and Jolie stepped inside. "I left my number on your desk. If you ever need anything, or have any questions, please call. Owen is a great employer. You'll really enjoy working for him."

"I think you're right. Thanks, Jolie."

She smiled. "I'm sure I'll see you around town."

Ronnie imagined they would run into each other occasionally in this small town. She also imagined it was tough keeping a secret around here.

An hour later a very pregnant woman pushed through the front door of Owen's office. Even though the snow from Monday had moved east and the sun was shining, freezing temperatures had settled over the area. The chill swept in and swirled around Ronnie like a mini tornado. The woman was carrying a small bouquet wrapped in a protective covering. She set the flowers on the corner of the reception desk and unwound a scarf to reveal a smile that lit her whole face. "Hi. I'm Alex McCreed."

"I'm Ronnie Coleman," Ronnie said, standing and shaking the woman's extended hand.

"I feel like we know each other already."

Ronnie shook her head. "I don't think we've ever met."

Alex waved a hand. "I mean from the chitchat. Gossip is an important form of entertainment in small towns. I know you drive a white Toyota that was in Klein's Auto Shop—hope the repair was quick and inexpensive. I know you met Rita at the post office—sorry about that, by the way. I know you're pretty—seems you made quite an impression on Max Klein. And according to Lily Johnson you already have a library card."

Ronnie laughed. Her thought about not being able to keep secrets in this town was apparently spot-on. "I did have my car in the repair shop and the repair was quick and inexpensive. I remember meeting Lily at the library, but I don't know the other two people you just mentioned."

"Rita works at the post office. She said you came to her rescue Monday morning when Kevin Klein was roughing her up."

Ah, the guy who thought it was okay to park in the drive-thru lane. "He's a Klein too?"

Alex removed the protective covering from the bouquet. "Yes. You have to understand, Kevin would never rough anyone up. And Max is the brother who was in the office when you picked up your car."

"So, Nate and Kevin and Max own Klein's?"

"There are actually five brothers, but yes, the three oldest own the shop."

Ronnie filed away the information. If she was going to live here, she should learn people's names. She indicated the flowers. "Are these for Owen?"

"No, they're for you."

She turned the bouquet, looking for a card from her parents, but didn't spot one. "Who sent them?"

"Me. They're a welcome-to-Eden-Falls bouquet. The

meaning of a daffodil is lasting friendship—which I hope we'll have—and lavender stands for the promise of new adventure."

Lasting friendship and new adventure, she liked that. "Besides red roses, I didn't know flowers stood for anything."

"In the strict Victorian era, floriography, or the language of plants, was used to convey messages."

"Did you take classes in flori-og-raphy?" she asked, stumbling over the word.

"No. I inherited Pretty Posies from my grandmother and she taught me."

Ronnie touched the delicate tip of a daffodil. "Well, thank you. It's been a long time since anyone gave me flowers. They'll brighten up the office." She stole a glance at Alex's middle. "When are you due?"

"Two weeks."

"And you're delivering flowers? Shouldn't you be home with your feet up or something?"

Alex laughed. "You sound like my husband."

"That I sound like a husband is something I never thought I'd hear."

Alex laughed harder, then crossed her legs. "Oh, don't make me laugh—I'll pee."

That made Ronnie laugh.

"I better get back to the shop." She headed for the door, then turned back. "Hey, I'm meeting friends at Rowdy's Bar and Grill tomorrow night at seven. You're welcome to join us. In fact, I insist. It will be a great way for you to meet some more of the townspeople."

The thought of meeting women her age was exciting. Besides Owen, she really didn't know anyone yet. "I'd love to come. Thanks for the invite."

"I heard you're living at Mrs. O'Malley's. She's a sweetheart. You'll love her. Jillian, one of the girls you'll meet tomorrow, used to live in that same apartment."

"Mrs. O'Malley is sweet."

"Rowdy's is a block off the square." Alex rewound her scarf and gave a wave. "I'll see you tomorrow."

"Thanks again for the welcome bouquet."

The rest of the afternoon breezed by. Owen was in court in the nearby town of Harrisville, so she had the office to herself. She cleaned out the fridge and spent some time straightening the reception area, which was already immaculate.

It was nice to work in such a cozy space rather than the commercial buildings she was used to. Each room in the Victorian house had been turned into usable space. The walls were paneled in walnut, and the whole house was decorated with rich, warm colors and beautiful antiques. The foyer served as the reception area. The dining room now held a conference table and chairs. The library, with its beautiful bay window overlooking the side yard, was Owen's office. Before he left for court, Owen told Ronnie she could convert the small sitting room into her office when he hired a new receptionist after the first of the year.

Her very own office.

He'd also told her an events planner had just bought and remodeled the Victorian next door. She was going to use part of the house for a tea and sandwich shop, which would be convenient for a quick lunch. A real estate office was scheduled to move into the second floor soon.

Owen was still in Harrisville when she locked up the office for the night. She'd noticed East Winds Chinese restaurant when she drove around the square this morning and decided to go there for dinner.

Inside, the restaurant was warm and the smells enticing. She asked for a table close to the window so she could look out over her new town. As soon as she ordered, her phone buzzed with a message. She expected it to be from her mom —the fourth today. Instead she felt the ridiculous thump of her heart when she glanced at the screen and saw the mysterious stranger's number.

Can you talk?

East Winds was too busy to hold a conversation. Not really. I'm in a restaurant.

What's for dinner?"

Chinese.

Something we have in common. Chinese is one of my favorites.

Mine, too! sounded too . . . eager, chirpy, needy. Ronnie deleted the exclamation mark before hitting *Send*.

A long minute passed and he didn't respond, so she scrolled to her mom's number and quickly texted, Had a great day. After dinner, I'm going to climb into a warm tub. I'll call tomorrow.

When the waiter set a steaming plate in front of her, she put her phone aside. Leaning over, she took a deep breath and savored the rich, sweet aroma of General Tso's chicken. Perfect dinner on a cold night.

Her phone buzzed.

Sorry. I had a customer picking up their car. How is yours running?

Good. Everyone around highly recommends the shop I used.

Word of mouth is the best advertisement. You have a good day?

Yes. Busy. You?

Same. Still like the new boss?

Owen was the best boss she'd ever had. He's great.

What did you order for dinner?

General Tso's chicken.

Ah, another one of my favorites.

Ronnie smiled. Another thing she and mystery man had in common.

~

Kevin tried to imagine her face as they texted back and forth. All he had was a voice to go on. Did she have dark hair? Blonde? Was it short or long? Was she petite? Tall? Blue eyes? Brown? Maybe green? Where did she live? What did she drive? So many questions tumbled through his mind.

Is she a cheerful person, or on the pessimistic side? Is she close to her family or independent? A loner or surrounded by friends? Sweet or snarky? Is she dating someone? Married? The last two were important questions, ones he should ask if he was going to continue texting.

Are you married?

LOL. No. Are you?

Good answer, he thought. No, not married. Dating someone?

Nope.

Another good answer. Something else we have in common.

Ugh! We sound pathetic.

"Hey, Kevin," Max said, pushing through the garage bay door before Kevin had a chance to type out a response. "Put synthetic 5W-20 on the next order. We're almost out."

"Full synthetic or synthetic blend?"

"Both."

Max jotted a note on a pad of paper with *Klein's Auto Shop* printed on the bottom. His phone dinged a message.

Did I lose you?

No, and we're not pathetic. We're selective.

Nice comeback.

He wondered if she was smiling, maybe even laughing under her breath at their conversation. Two people who had never seen each other, getting acquainted via mobile devices. Not exactly the way he liked to get to know a woman, but in this day and age…

Gotta sign off now. My dinner's getting cold.

Talk tomorrow?

She sent him a smiling emoji.

After he locked up the auto shop, Kevin drove to his mom and stepdad's farmhouse at the edge of town. They were busy with details for the church bazaar, and he'd promised to help with the decorations. His mom wanted him to cut profile images of the nativity figures from sheets of plywood, and for him the cutting was easy if someone else drew the images. Art wasn't his forte.

He entered the kitchen and took a deep breath. His mom's cooking, which was the best around, would be a scent to contain and sell. Heaven in a bottle.

"Hi, honey," his mom said. She set a big pan of lasagna on the stovetop. "You're just in time."

"I agree. That smells delicious."

"Isadora Adams came over earlier and drew the nativity images on the plywood. Can you get those cut out after dinner?"

Kevin shed his coat. "That's what I'm here for. Your lasagna is a bonus. Let me wash my hands and I'll set the table."

He could hear his mom humming while he washed up in the bathroom off the kitchen. She was his rock. Always had been. A single parent for years after their dad abandoned them, she'd raised five boys alone. Working two—sometimes three—jobs to put food on the table. Until Murray came along, she'd struggled and worried alone. Then Murray relieved the boatload of anxiety five active kids created. He'd bought this piece of property with plenty of outdoor space where growing, rambunctious kids could run and explore, and a house big enough for them all.

"How's business?" his mom asked when he came back into the kitchen.

"Great."

"And how are *you*?"

He glanced at his mother, who rested a hip against the counter, arms crossed. "I'm good," he said.

"Seeing anyone?"

"No. Well…" He couldn't help the smile. "Maybe. In a roundabout way."

She laughed. Through all their growing-up years, despite all she'd gone through, his mom was always one to enjoy laughter. She could always find something to smile about, something to appreciate. "What does that mean?"

"I called the wrong number when I was looking for Ethan on Monday, and ever since, 'wrong number' and I have been texting."

A frown creased her brow. "You've been texting with a woman over the phone and that's called seeing someone nowadays?"

"Technically, we're not seeing each other, but—"

"Son, do you know anything about her? What if she's underage?"

"She doesn't sound underage." He heard the defensiveness in his voice and was sure his mom did too.

Blowing out a breath, she walked close and looked up into his eyes. "Honey, what if she's married?"

"She's not. I asked. She also said she's not dating anyone."

"And you believe her?"

"Why would she lie?"

Shaking her head, his mom straightened the already

perfect tablecloth. "What if she lives in Florida or Maine or London?"

"She has Ethan's old phone number. A Washington area code."

"Which means nothing. Maybe her parents live in Washington and she's at school in Virginia or Oklahoma."

"She said she started a new job on Monday, so she's not in school."

"Because no student works their way through school."

"This isn't like you, to look for the negative."

His mom cupped his face. "Just be careful. Relationships are hard enough without adding more complications. And texting is no way to get to know someone. You need to hear her voice, look into her eyes."

He wanted to brush his mom's concerns aside. The woman hadn't sounded underage, yet that was something he should be concerned about. He'd ask her the next time they talked.

When she'd said she wasn't married or dating, he believed her, just as she seemed to believe him. But they both could have lied and the other wouldn't know. The same went for meeting someone face-to-face. You were never really sure if what they said was true or something they made up for that occasion.

Which was why he despised the dating life.

He finished setting the table as the first doubts settled around his heart.

CHAPTER 4

*R*onnie spent Friday researching a case for Owen. It felt good—better than good—to be doing research on top of answering phones, making copies, and filing away papers. Until Owen hired a receptionist, she still manned the front desk. Both jobs kept her busy, something she'd never minded, since being busy moved the day along quicker.

Plus, she was reasonably excited—and a little nervous—to meet Alex and her friends tonight.

She closed the Washington policies and procedures book and opened the rules of evidence book for the state. Since both her parents were science geniuses, they had pushed her in the same direction, but her interests had always veered toward law. Education was only one of the many areas of her life where her parents interfered. She understood that they thought they knew what was best, but at twenty-nine she was old enough to make decisions for herself. Something they were just learning to respect after she announced she'd taken a job in Eden Falls. Putting distance between them was the only way to draw her line in the sand and finally attain independence to pursue her area of interest.

She shut down her computer and got her purse out of the bottom drawer of the desk just as Owen came down the hall. "Thanks for your help this afternoon. Those two files you e-mailed were exactly what I was looking for." He shrugged into his overcoat. "Ready to go?"

"I'm meeting the woman who owns the flower shop and some of her friends at Rowdy's Bar and Grill."

"Ah, it will be good for you to get out and meet someone besides a stodgy attorney." He pushed his wire-frame glasses farther up on his nose and gestured toward the front door. "I'll lock up behind you. Oh! I've been meaning to mention all day. The church on Willow Street is having a huge bazaar tomorrow to raise funds for families in the area who need help for Christmas. If you're still looking for any books, cookware, art, that kind of thing, they'll have almost anything you might need. Or want."

That sounded like a good way to spend a cold, snowy Saturday. "Thanks for the info. I'll stop by."

A bazaar would also give her a chance to meet more people, and she could pick up some Christmas decorations for her apartment. This would be the first time she wouldn't be spending Christmas Eve at her parents' house, though they didn't know it yet. She imagined most people who moved away from family for the first time got homesick during the holidays and couldn't wait to get back for a visit, but she didn't think that would be the case for her. Though she'd had her own apartment in Spokane, her mom, or dad, or both, dropped by almost every day. Now she liked not worrying about a teacup in the sink or a throw she hadn't folded—nitpicky things her mom always noticed and never failed to mention.

She stopped by the grocery store for fresh vegetables,

hoping to make minestrone soup over the weekend since the temperatures were supposed to stay in the frigid zone. She also added a package of chicken breasts, a sweet potato, and two different flavors of Ben and Jerry's to her cart—a girl needed her ice cream, which she'd count as her dairy—then dropped in salad fixings to even out her unbalanced diet. With the move and new job, she hadn't had time to look for a gym. She'd ask the girls tonight if there was one in town.

At her apartment, she unloaded her groceries, checked in with Mrs. O'Malley, then changed into jeans and a sweater. Not for the first time, she wished her small space had a fireplace to cut the basement's chill. She pulled on a pair of knee boots and ventured back out into the cold.

The interior of Rowdy's was warm, wood rustic, and surprisingly busy. The tantalizing smell of something coming from the kitchen made her stomach growl. Country music played in the background, loud enough to hear, but not so loud you couldn't hold a conversation. She glanced around, hoping to spot Alex—otherwise she wouldn't know who to look for.

A tall, handsome man with a ponytail and a tray of drinks approached. He balanced the tray and leaned in close. "Hi, I'm Rowdy. Are you Ronnie?"

"I am," she said, surprised he knew her name.

"Alex called to say she's running a little late and to keep an eye out for you. Follow me and I'll introduce you to her girl-gang."

"I like your place."

"Thanks. Alex said you just moved here."

"From Spokane," she said when he glanced back at her.

"Welcome to Eden Falls."

"Thank you."

Four women sat at a table. Rowdy introduced Stella as his

wife, a redhead named Carolyn, and a pretty woman named Jillian as he placed their drinks in front of them.

Jolie waved from the opposite side of the table. "Hi, Ronnie. I'm glad Alex invited you."

It was nice to see a familiar face. Ronnie wasn't an introvert, but felt completely out of place meeting a group of women who'd probably been friends forever.

"What can I get you to drink?" Rowdy asked.

"I'll take a ginger ale."

"Coming right up. Alex's platter of nachos will be out in a few minutes."

"Alex always orders a giant platter of nachos for our girls' night out," Jillian explained.

"Tell us about yourself," Stella asked as soon as her husband walked away.

"Not much to tell. I just moved here from Spokane."

"She started working for Owen on Monday," Jolie added.

Ronnie turned to Jillian. "Alex told me I moved into your old apartment."

Jillian smiled. "Oh, you'll love Mrs. O'Malley. That basement is a little dark, but I loved it anyway."

"If you don't mind me asking, why did you move?"

"I got married and my husband had a house."

Good to know. "Congratulations."

Someone stopped at her elbow and Ronnie looked up at a gorgeous woman. She had deep sapphire eyes and long hair that was so black it had a blue cast.

"Who's this?" she asked, not unkindly, but without a note of welcome in her voice.

"Ronnie Coleman, meet Misty Garrett, the mean girl of our group."

"Would you quit introducing me that way, Stella? I'm nice now," Misty growled. "Most of the time." Misty glanced at her. "Your mom named you Ronnie?"

"And there she is," Stella said on a laugh.

"Ronnie is short for Veronica, and my mom hates the shortened version." Luckily, Alex chose that moment to join them. She gave Ronnie a quick hug. "I'm so glad you could come. You've all met Ronnie?"

"Misty has made her usual first impression."

"Shut up, Stella," Misty hissed.

Jillian frowned at Stella. "Why do you goad her?"

"Payback for all her years of cruelty. I lost count of how many boyfriends she stole."

"They weren't worth keeping if she could steal them," Carolyn said.

While they chatted, Ronnie began to understand the dynamic among the six friends. They filled her in on some of the people and places in town. The worst part of moving from Spokane had been leaving her lifetime girlfriends behind. The best part of finding a job in Eden Falls? They were only a few hours away. A girls' weekend would be easy to plan.

"Hi, sister-in-law."

Ronnie recognized the guy from the auto shop. Alex had said his name was Max.

With hands on Jolie's shoulders, he looked around their table. "Hello, ladies." His eyes stopped on Ronnie. "And the new girl in town. Veronica, right?"

"Good memory."

"I never forget a pretty face."

Stella snorted out a laugh—her third for the night. "Really, Max. Does that line ever work for you?"

He winked at Stella. "It worked on you."

"Yeah, in tenth grade. Time to come up with something new, buddy."

"I see marriage hasn't sweetened your snark." He flashed a smile at her before sauntering off.

Misty glanced from Max to Ronnie. "You could do worse. Max is cute."

Ronnie shook her head. "I just moved and started a new job, so I'm not looking to jump into a romance right now."

Alex laughed. "Famous last words. Magic always happens when you're not looking. And Christmas is such a magical time."

She knew Stella was married to Rowdy, and both Jillian and Alex had mentioned husbands. "Are you all married?"

"All within the past two years." Stella nudged Ronnie's ginger ale closer. "Don't drink the water if you don't want to end up walking down the aisle."

"Did you leave someone behind in Spokane?" Carolyn asked.

"A lot of someones." All eyes turned her way. This time Misty snorted.

"That came out wrong. I just mean I've dated a lot, but there's no one special. My last boyfriend transferred with his job a few months ago." He'd asked her to move with him, but there was no mention of a ring or forever. "I've never come close to walking down the aisle."

Alex laughed. "You better stop talking or we'll be planning a wedding by the end of the month."

"Not for me. I'm going to enjoy the single life for a while."

She glanced up when a huge plate of nachos was set in the middle of the table.

"Rowdy asked me to drop this with you. I told him there was a delivery fee."

Ronnie recognized the guy from the post office. The one who parked in the drive-thru lane. He also set a stack of small plates on the table, picked up the top one, and loaded it with nachos. She couldn't believe the nerve of the guy. He didn't even ask. Who did he think he was? She was surprised when none of the women said a thing about his poor manners, and just accepted his behavior.

"Ronnie, this is Kevin Klein, Casanova-Max's big brother," Stella said.

"I was just going to introduce myself and ask if he needed a bigger plate," Ronnie said, narrowing her gaze on Kevin. "I can get you one if you'd like."

~

Kevin glanced at the new girl and immediately recognized the blue of her eyes. The woman from the post office. "This plate is big enough, and we've already met."

A glimmer of recognition—something about the guy—fired in the back of her mind, but she brushed it aside. "We didn't actually meet. We bumped into each other. I see your manners haven't improved."

"Well, it's only been a few days. Can't expect miracles so quickly." He glanced around the table. "Enjoy your evening, ladies."

He headed back to where his brother sat. Max had no idea what he'd be up against with that one. He'd have his hands full. *Good luck, bro.*

He bellied up to the bar and slapped his brother on the shoulder. "You sure know how to pick 'em. That Veronica is something. Gotta hand it to you for calling dibs."

"Actually, I met someone online this week, so if you want her…"

"You do realize she's a person and you can't just give her away, right?"

"I'm not giving her away, just recanting my dibs. She's all yours."

"Who are we giving away?" bartender Mike Stettler asked as he set a drink in front of Kevin.

"The girl sitting at Alex's table," Max motioned toward Alex and her friends. "She's new in town and Kevin's interested."

"I'm not interested."

"You just said, 'That Veronica is something.'"

He glanced at his brother. "I did, but I didn't mean it in a good way. More in an I'd-rather-have-chicken-pox-than-date-her way."

Max grimaced as his gaze floated behind Kevin.

"Really?" came a voice from behind him. "Chicken pox rather than a plague? I'm a little disappointed. All this time I thought I was more formidable than chicken pox."

Kevin closed his eyes. "You weren't supposed to hear that."

"Obviously." The woman stepped between him and his brother. "I knew you were a peach when I saw you Monday morning jostling a little old lady."

"You were jostling a lady?" Mike asked with raised eyebrows.

"Rita."

Max waved a hand. "No explanation necessary."

Kevin turned toward Blue-eyes. "I wasn't jostling, or, as Rita put it, manhandling her. I was helping her to the door of the post office so she wouldn't slip on the ice. I hadn't planned to park in the drive-thru lane, but when she got out of my car, she said it was slippery, so I parked and walked her to the door. There was no jostling or manhandling involved."

"She said—"

"That's just Rita. We take most of what she says with a grain of salt," Max said.

Blue-eyes glanced at Mike for confirmation and he nodded.

"Happy?" Kevin asked her.

She set her jaw in obstinance. "Can I get another ginger ale, please?"

"Not into admitting when you're wrong?"

"I'm not sure I am wrong."

Squawk!

Ronnie sloshed the drink Mike had just handed her.

Kevin passed her a napkin off the bar. "Well, hi there, Rita. Meet Veronica."

Rita leaned forward and peered through her thick-lensed glasses. "Veronica what?"

"I go by Ronnie. Ronnie Coleman."

Rita tilted her head at an odd angle, in that birdlike habit of hers. "I don't know any Colemans."

"I'm not from here. I moved from Spokane."

"I don't know any Colemans in Spokane."

Ronnie's eyes darted from Rita to him, her look screaming *help!* He tried not to smirk while enjoying every second of her discomfort, until the thought of his mom pushed through his gloating. If she was here, she'd flick his ear until it was beet red, her favorite form of punishment. "She's from the Elk Range Colemans, Rita. They own lots of land on that side of the state."

Although it didn't seem possible, Rita's eyes got bigger. "That right? Well, Elk Range Colemans are welcome in Eden Falls anytime." She glanced Kevin up and down, then did the same to Max. "Maybe you need to rethink the company you keep, though. Both these boys are bad to the core. Nate's the man you should go after. He's the good brother."

"He's also the married brother, Rita," Max said. "His wife is sitting right over there. Remember Jolie and their baby girl, Riley?"

Squawk! "Pity." Rita walked away.

Ronnie sloshed her drink again, this time down Kevin's pants.

Mike placed more napkins on the bar and Kevin mopped at his wet jeans. "Thanks for that."

"She scared me," Ronnie said. "Does she always make loud screeching noises?"

"She flaps her arms a lot too," Max said.

Veronica narrowed her eyes at him. "You just lied to that woman. There's no such thing as the Elk Range in Spokane."

"You're welcome," Kevin said.

Miss Hoity-Toity Hotshot turned in a huff and marched back to the table without another word.

"What did you do to piss her off?" Max asked.

"Helped an old lady to the door."

Squawk! "Who are you calling old?"

"Sorry, Rita." Kevin glared at his brother. "You could have warned me she was within hearing distance."

Max chuckled. "And miss all this fun?"

Kevin tugged out his phone. No messages. His anonymous friend was probably out with friends…or a date…or her husband. *Thanks for planting those thoughts, Mom.*

He scrolled to her number. "Are you planning to actually get together with this online girl?"

"Yep. Tomorrow night in South Fork."

"Good luck." Kevin texted. Friday night. Are you out and about?

After several minutes his phone buzzed with a new message. Yes. Out with some new friends. You?

Having a drink with my brother but heading home. I have an early morning.

Don't drink and drive.

Never. Talk tomorrow?

I'd love to. Have a good night.

You too.

Kevin stuffed his phone into a pocket and shrugged into his coat.

"You heading out?" Max asked.

"Yep. I promised Mom I'd help her set up for the church bazaar tomorrow morning." He lifted a hand. "See ya, Mike."

Not sure why, but he glanced at the table where Blue-eyes sat. She was laughing at something one of the girls said. Max was right, she was pretty, but way too judgmental, especially about subjects she knew nothing about.

CHAPTER 5

When Ronnie arrived the next morning, she followed the signs directing shoppers around to the church's fellowship hall doors on the side of the building. Inside was a beehive of activity. She closed her eyes and inhaled, enjoying the smells of popcorn, fresh bread, and chili, tempting her to try them all.

Three back-to-back aisles of booths were set up. She spotted Christmas decorations, jams and jellies, homemade soup mixes, winter scarves, and mittens. A sign on the left directed kids to a separate area where a cupcake walk and other games were set up.

Ready for some serious shopping and eating, she shoved her gloves into a pocket, unwound her scarf, and shrugged out of her coat, which she hung in a coatroom off to the side. The first booth she visited was filled with shelves of girly-scented soaps that smelled heavenly. She picked up one after the other, breathing in deeply. Of course she had to have one. How to choose? Freesia won. But the grapefruit came in at such a close second, she bought both.

Next she ducked into a booth lined with crazy socks.

She picked out a striped pair, another with hippos, and a third pair covered with colorful hearts. A bracelet across the aisle caught her eye. She went over and slipped it onto her arm. It looked too perfect to take off, so she untwisted the tag, paid the cute girl with rings dangling from each nostril —*hate to see what shows up after a sneeze*—and moved down the aisle.

She found a wreath at the next booth that would look great on her door. After paying for it, Ronnie talked the woman into holding it until she was finished shopping.

The next booth had tables lined with homemade breads. She picked up a loaf of banana nut and sniffed. *Yep. One of these.*

A woman wearing an apron embroidered with a loaf of bread stopped in front of her. "You like banana nut?"

"I would like a loaf of every choice, but my jeans would protest." She picked up another loaf. "Oh, orange cranberry."

"Are you buying gifts?"

Ronnie held up her bags. "No, just indulging in stuff I don't need but love. Do you think I could slice the bread and freeze the slices separately?"

"Yes."

"Then I'll take a loaf of plain white too."

The lady laughed.

Something about her looked familiar. Maybe her smile or the crinkle of her eyes. The sound of her laugh.

"Do you live in the area?" the woman asked.

"I just moved to Eden Falls last weekend."

She took the loaves of bread from Ronnie. "How do you like it here?"

"So far I love it. The town is picturesque, and the people are so friendly." Ronnie pulled out her wallet. "Are you from Eden Falls?"

"Born and raised and married." She stopped next to a

small cash register. "And had five kids and divorced and remarried."

"Wow. That's a mouthful."

"Kind of was." The woman smiled and held out her hand. "I'm Irene Klein."

Irene's two-fisted handshake was firm, warm, and welcoming. "Klein as in Klein's Auto Shop?"

"Ah, you must have met at least one of my boys already."

Yep, I met Mr. Annoying. "Max and Kevin. Unfortunately, my car decided to act up Monday morning. Fortunately, their auto shop was close and they were able to fix it quickly. I'm Ronnie Coleman."

"Oh, you work for Owen." She smiled when Ronnie nodded. "Small town. I'm sure you've heard my daughter-in-law worked for Owen before she had my first grandbaby."

"I actually met Jolie and her friends at Rowdy's last night."

"Fun. Those girls have been friends forever." Irene punched a few keys on the little register. "So, tell me about yourself, Ronnie."

That seemed to be the standard question asked by people in Eden Falls. "Except for college, I've lived in Spokane all my life. When I saw Owen was looking for help, I applied, and here I am."

"Are you married?"

"Nope, single." Ronnie pulled some bills from her wallet. "I'm looking forward to this yummy bread."

"I'm making this loaf of white a welcome-to-Eden-Falls gift."

"Oh, I couldn't—"

Irene nodded firmly. "You most certainly can. You take it and enjoy."

"Thank you. That's really kind."

Irene waved her thanks away. "I hope you like it here."

"I'm sure I will." Ronnie put her purchases into one of the

bags she already carried. "I noticed several booths selling jam. Do you have a recommendation?"

"Absolutely." Irene pointed down the aisle to a Saunders' Orchards banner. "Amy's blackberry jam will make you weep with pleasure. You probably met Jillian last night."

"I did."

"Amy is Jillian's mom."

Despite her dislike for Kevin, Ronnie really liked his mom. "Well, if I'm going to be weeping, I hope they sell tissues too."

Irene laughed and pulled her into an unexpected hug at the same time. "Come back and see me. I have tissues."

Ronnie was surprised by Irene's friendliness to a stranger. In fact, the whole town had been so welcoming. Her stiff, authoritative parents would be guarded in this happy place. She walked away from the booth with a wave and immediately spotted Kevin standing across the aisle watching. She turned in the opposite direction.

Kevin had watched Ronnie since she walked into the fellowship hall. The lunatic visited and bought something at almost every booth. She carried more bags than a bellman.

"She's sweet."

He glanced at his mom, who smiled like an alligator eyeing lunch. "Is she?"

"And funny."

When?

"And pretty."

Okay, she had him on that one. "She bought some bread?"

"Two loaves. I gave her a third as a gift. She asked if she could freeze the slices separately, which is very resourceful."

"Numbering her virtues, Ma?"

"No, just telling you the few things I noticed about her in a very short time. She said she's single. Perfect for Max, don't you think? I can picture them together."

Max? "He told me last night he met someone online."

She glanced at him from the corner of her eye. "Is that how it's done these days? Online, texting—can't you boys meet a nice girl face-to-face?"

"Eden Falls is small. There aren't enough single women to go around."

"Funny, the single women in town are probably saying the same thing." She pulled a basket from under one of the tables and replenished the loaves Ronnie had bought. "How is your wrong number romance going?"

It wasn't. "We haven't talked for several days. Texts only."

"You can't get to know a woman or girl—since you really have no idea how old she is—with texts."

"Not true. I know she likes Chinese—General Tso's chicken, to be specific. What else is there to know?"

"What color are her eyes? Her hair? Does she treat her mother well? Does she have any siblings? Is she kind? Is she dating someone? Also important, where does she live? Hopefully in the western side of the United States. Even better if she's in Washington state—unless she's a murderer—"

"Ma—"

"—or travels with the circus. She might be the knife thrower. Wonder if she ever misses? If she breathes fire, you won't have to worry about buying any more lighters or matches. Just prop her up in front of the logs in the fireplace and say, 'Hit it!'"

My mother the comedian. "Okay. Enough." He nodded toward her booth. "You have a couple of customers. Need some help?"

"Absolutely not. Go. Have fun." She turned him by the

shoulders in the direction Ronnie had gone. "Meet a pretty girl who can look you in the eye. Use your Klein charm to put a smile on her face."

"No matchmaking, Ma. Blue-eyes and I, we don't exactly get along."

"Impossible. She's adorable, and so personable. Obviously you've noticed her gorgeous blue eyes and that smile is—"

"Bye," he said, turning his back and walking away.

He stopped at the kids' corner and watched the littles rounding a circle of chairs while Christmas songs played from speakers. When the music stopped, the kids scrambled onto the closest chair. The one left standing had to leave the circle. One girl broke into tears when she couldn't find a chair. Patsy Douglas quickly defused the situation by offering a candy cane. She set the basket of shepherd's crooks on a table nearby. He reached for one, only to have his hand slapped. He flinched and dropped the candy cane.

"Those are for the children."

He slowly turned toward the crazy lady. "Did you just slap me?"

"Oh, please," Ronnie moaned on an exhale. "I'm pretty sure you'll live. Why are you stealing candy from children?"

"I'm not stealing. I was going to take a piece from that big basketful."

"So in other words, you were stealing." She shifted her weight from one foot to the other, a smug look on her face. "Were you just going to fill your pockets like you filled your plate last night?"

"What are you so uptight about? It's a bite-size candy cane."

"That someone bought for the children, not the grownups."

Tired of being on the defensive, he decided to turn the

conversation around by nodding toward her bags. "Are you trying to buy the place out?"

Her blue eyes flashed. "What business is it of yours what I buy? Oh, right. None."

"It's as much my business as me taking a candy cane is yours."

She huffed out a breath. "Huge difference."

"Are you finished shopping?"

"Actually, I think I'll go for round two. I need more bread."

"You have three loaves."

She took a step back, the skin between her brows puckering. "You're spying on me?"

"I wasn't spying." *Watching, yes.* "I was headed to my mom's booth to see if she needed any help, spotted you, and, since we don't exactly get along, I decided to wait until you were finished stocking up."

Her pretty eyes widened. "Mighty nice of you."

"Was that a compliment?"

The corner of her mouth twitched. "I guess, in a round-about, I-still-don't-think-I-like-you kind of way."

"Huh." Touching her shoulder, he steered her out of the way of two anxious kids trying to get into the cakewalk fun. "Most people like me."

"Really?" she asked with a hundred watts of exaggeration.

"Love me, in fact. Say I'm endearing. Want some caramel corn?"

The skin between her brows puckered again. "What?"

"I asked if you'd like some caramel corn. Not a hard question. A simple yes will get you a bag."

"Yes." She narrowed her eyes. "Why are you being nice all of a sudden?"

"I'm always nice." Again, he turned her by the shoulders

toward a booth selling one of his favorite treats. "Two bags, please."

When he held out a bag for her, a smile flickered across her face. A alluring smile that caused funny things to happen in the vicinity of his heart.

"Thank you."

"You're welcome."

Her smile grew. "It's still warm."

"That's when it's the best."

She popped a piece into her mouth and closed her eyes. "Mmm, that's good."

Her purr of happiness stuttered his heartbeat.

Opening her eyes, she looked directly at him. "So, that was your mom in the bread booth."

"She makes the best bread in the county."

"She said she had five boys. What number are you?"

He chuckled. "One, of course."

Her brow crinkled for a third time. "You say with such honest arrogance."

"I'm the firstborn, but I can also say with confidence that she's always liked me best."

He circled the caramel corn booth, making sure she followed, and waved to a couple of plastic chairs nearby, surprised when she readily sat next to him. She set her packages at her feet and dug into the caramel corn.

"I can't imagine what it must have been like to be your mom in a house with five boys. Six counting your dad."

"My dad couldn't imagine it either, so he left."

"He left her alone to raise—" She covered her mouth with her hand. "Sorry, that was so rude of me."

"That's never stopped you before."

She looked at him with raised brows. "Oh! Good response. But seriously, I am sorry if what you said about your father is true."

He lifted a shoulder to shrug off her comment. "He left a long time ago. We survived. I like to think we're better for it."

"Five boys. Your mother must be a saint." She tipped her head back and dropped several pieces of caramel corn into her mouth.

"My mom is a saint, but only because that's her nature, not because we were a rotten bunch of boys."

"I bet that's what all rotten bunches of boys say."

"We weren't—"

She held up a finger. "Think very carefully before you commit perjury."

"My first impression of you was right," he said, with a shake of his head. "You're nuts."

"Ha!" she said, pointing a finger at his nose. "You're just saying that because I'm right."

"We weren't rotten. We *were* boys. We got into the same amount of trouble all boys get into. Sure, we fought and got yelled at and grounded, but we also did good things. We took care of Mom and helped clean the house and even cooked for her."

"Hot dogs and macaroni?"

"And Hamburger Helper to change things up. Sometimes tacos. Spaghetti was my specialty."

She raised her eyebrows. "Was?"

"Does it matter?"

"Not really." She went back to munching her caramel corn.

He had to admit he was enjoying their back-and-forth banter. She was quick. "What about you? Sisters? Brothers? Both?"

"None of the above."

"Ah, that explains everything. Only child, spoiled, bratty, always gets her way."

She slowly turned to glare at him. "You don't know anything about me."

"I know you jump to conclusions without knowing all the facts. Is that an only child thing, or just a Ronnie thing?"

"I'll admit I did jump to a few conclusions."

"A few? Everything between us has been assumed."

"There's nothing between us."

True.

She dumped the rest of her popcorn into his bag, gathered her packages, and stood. "People are staring, which means it's time for me to go before *they* start jumping to conclusions about *us*."

"We wouldn't want any conclusion jumping—especially about us."

"Exactly. Thanks for the caramel corn and the chat. It's been…enlightening."

Yes, it has. "See you around, Blue-eyes." The surprise on her face gave him a smidgeon of glowing satisfaction.

With nothing better to do, he watched her bop in and out of a few more booths before bundling up in coat and hat and heading out the door.

He tugged his phone from a pocket, wondering what his anonymous friend was doing today. He scrolled to her number and hit *Send*. Her phone rang three times before the call connected. "Hi."

The breathless voice stopped him, sending a bucket of cold water crashing over his head. *No!*

"Hello?"

Kevin disconnected the call.

CHAPTER 6

Kevin slipped his cell phone back into his pocket and leaned forward, elbows on his thighs, staring at the floor while reality settled in and hollowed out his chest.

The minute she answered the phone he knew. Anonymous Voice was Veronica Coleman. They were one and the same.

Out of all the phone numbers in all the world, how did she end up with Ethan's? Out of all the women in all the world he had happened to call—and connect with—the one woman who didn't like him. There was no way he and Blue-eyes… He couldn't even finish the thought.

He grabbed his coat and headed out into the cold, determined to snap out of the funk he'd put himself in. The day was too beautiful, the sky too blue, to feel such overwhelming disappointment, yet he did. He'd placed too much hope on a stupid phone call. Allowed a mysterious, sexy voice to plant a seed that would never push through the soil and see the light of day.

When he reached the turnoff for the shop, he continued

out of town until he found a dirt road that was cleared of snow enough to take him to the river. In the shallows along the edge the water had frozen, but in the middle the icy cold river flowed with purpose toward its ocean destination.

Silly how a simple revelation could plummet him into such a bad mood. A hawk lifted from high atop a pine and swooped down, probably in search of its next meal. Kevin pulled the bag of caramel corn out of his coat pocket and dumped the sweet treat on the ground for the birds and bunnies.

Thirty minutes later, he closed himself in the office at the shop and worked until it was time to help his mom dismantle her booth at the bazaar. As usual, she had no leftovers. Though the booth rental money went to helping families who couldn't have Christmas otherwise, his mom would also donate her earnings for the day. Because the same booth rental money—years ago—had helped her provide a Christmas for her own boys.

With the help of his stepdad, he took apart her booth. Halfway through, he felt eyes boring into him and glanced sideways. His mom was studying him in a way that made him feel seven again, fresh from the riverbank and covered with mud.

"What?"

She shook her head. "You were so happy earlier and now…something has changed. I'm just wondering what."

"How do you know I was happy?"

"I saw your face when you were sitting over there with Ronnie, eating caramel corn."

He scoffed. "You didn't hear the conversation we were having. She's definitely not interested. And I have to say the feeling is—"

His mother pressed fingers to his lips. "Don't say something you can't take back."

He stopped. His mom was right, as usual. No need to express his thoughts aloud. What he didn't understand was how he could be so intrigued by someone on the phone, but that same person—and he was positive they were the same person—could be so judgmental and unlikeable when face-to-face. Which wasn't exactly true. They'd had a brief but civil conversation earlier.

"Sit," his mom said, pointing to a chair.

"Ma—"

His mom and stepdad exchanged a look before she pointed to the chair again.

Kevin blew out a breath and sat, knowing she wouldn't relent until she had her say.

She pulled another chair close. "What's going on?"

"Nothing. I'm fine."

She took his hand between hers. "Tell me what's going on, son. My oldest, my heart, my life," she said, resorting to the same sweet talk she used whenever one of her sons had a heavy heart. She turned his hand over and massaged his callused palm with the pad of her thumb. "What has you so down when you were smiling earlier?"

"I found out who the mystery voice is today."

"And you're disappointed because she lives in Florida and trains dolphins? No, she's a fortune cookie writer—you know that you can make very good money coming up with those fortunes?" She smiled. "Don't look at me like that. You know I'm only having fun."

"The girl I've been texting with is the same girl you think is so sweet and pretty."

Several expressions passed over her face before a laugh burst out like and explosion.

"Okay, not the reaction I expected, but you do like a good joke. Glad I can entertain you."

"You've got to give me this one," she said, wiping the

laugh-tears from her eyes. "You were so sure the girl on the phone was special and the one in front of you today wasn't. Open your eyes to the possibility that maybe, just maybe, Ronnie is special too."

Kevin shook his head. "No. This is one time you're wrong, Ma. We've argued every time we've been around each other. About everything."

"Of course none of the arguments between you could have been your fault, right?" she said, a smirk turning up the corners of her mouth.

"No. They came about because Ronnie's judgmental and assumes—" He threw his hands up in the air. "And you're laughing again."

"I'm sorry, but you're making too much out of something that's so silly."

"Silly. You should hear some of the things she's said to me. And she doesn't even know me." Even to his own ears, his argument sounded juvenile.

"So, change that. Let her get to know you."

A hand fell on his shoulder and he looked into his stepdad's face.

"Can I make a suggestion? Not sure it will work, but it might be worth a try."

Kevin dropped his head with a sigh. He'd hear the idea, store it away, and forget this whole conversation. Ronnie Coleman was impossible. No way could they work things out. "Sure, Murray, what do you have in mind?"

"This started with calling a wrong number, but you haven't been able to talk so you've been texting, right?"

He nodded, head still down. He should have known his mom would share with his stepdad. Not that it really mattered. Murray wouldn't go around town telling everyone.

"You know who she is, but she doesn't know who you are, so keep texting. I agree with your mother that isn't the best way to get to know each other, but I'm sure it has been done. Your mother loves that movie *Sleepless in Seattle*, and it's based on the same premise, only with e-mail."

"The movie is *You've Got Mail*, but same actress, honey. Good job," his mom said.

Murray chuckled. "Right. *You've Got Mail*. Cute girly movie. You should watch it sometime."

Kevin glanced up at Murray. "You want me to watch a movie?"

"Can't hurt," Murray said with a shrug. "And maybe it'll help."

"Oh, Kevin, open yourself up to new possibilities," his mom said. "Take a chance. When was the last time you stepped out of your comfort zone?"

Something he didn't do often. "Okay. I'll watch the movie. Thanks, Murray."

His mom laughed again. "That wasn't what I meant by stepping out of your comfort zone."

He pushed up to his feet. "No, but it's a start."

~

*R*onnie glanced at her phone for the tenth time since getting home from the bazaar. Mystery Man had called, but when she answered, no one was on the other end. Her reception wasn't the greatest in Eden Falls, but even in her basement apartment she had two bars. Plenty for a phone call. Maybe he was the one with the horrible reception.

She paced her tiny living room, feeling claustrophobic. After half a bag of caramel popcorn, dinner should be healthy, but suddenly she was slipping on her boots, grabbing a jacket, and heading out for a burger at Noelle's Café.

She walked the few blocks to Town Square as a light

snow started falling. The world was quiet and beautiful, a Norman Rockwell setting. She stuck out her gloved palm, watching while fat flakes settled and melted just as fast. Wouldn't it be nice to share this moment with someone?

She pulled out her phone and considered calling Mystery Man.

Geez! She hated it when that kind of thought popped into her mind. She was fine on her own, and didn't need a man to enjoy special moments.

For a long time after she went to college in Pullman, she felt she needed someone to fill the void her parents left when they weren't hovering. Boyfriend after boyfriend, she expected something they couldn't give.

Once she realized she needed to fill that void for herself, she began to enjoy her own company, savored her alone time. Still, there were moments like this when she wished she had someone with her to share the beauty.

She walked past the huge pine in the square, now covered with snow, the colorful lights glowing through. The decorated shops looked postcard perfect. She brushed the flakes off her shoulders and shook off her knit hat under Noelle's awning. When she pushed through the door of Noelle's, the heat enveloped her.

"Can I get a seat by the window?" Ronnie asked a waitress standing at the cash register.

"Sure. How about over there?" She motioned toward a vacant booth. "I'll bring a menu and some water."

Ronnie unbundled and hung her coat on the rack by the door, then took her seat. The waitress set a menu and a glass of water on the table.

"Actually, I know what I want."

"Perfect." She pulled an order pad and pencil from an apron pocket.

"I'll take a mushroom Swiss burger with fries and a hot chocolate."

"I'll put your order in."

"Thanks." She nearly dropped her phone when it buzzed with a text.

Hi. Sorry about earlier.

She stared at the message a moment. No explanation. But a sorry. She typed Not a problem and hit send.

How was your day?

She smiled. Expensive.

Yeah? How expensive? Or is that too personal?

No. I went to a church bazaar and kind of went crazy. Soap, socks, some cute Christmas decorations. Now I just need to get a tree.

Real or fake?

Absolutely real. I love the smell of pine trees. You?

Real all the way.

Something else they had in common. She felt silly texting back and forth like this was some kind of relationship when she didn't even know the guy. But it felt weirdly safe. And comfortable.

What did Mystery Man look like? What color were his eyes, his hair? Was he tall or shorter than she was? That might be weird. She liked to wear heels. Would he feel intimidated if she towered over him? Too many questions about someone she only knew through texts.

She could understand why people became friends over the Internet. There were few expectations. But there were also many questions. She wasn't sure she'd ever feel safe meeting him in person.

A sudden picture of Kevin Klein and his expressive eyes popped into her mind. After asking a question, he had a way of watching intensely while she answered.

You there?

Lost in thought, she glanced down at her phone. She'd missed him asking what she was doing. I'm at a cute little café for dinner. Mushroom swiss burger and hot chocolate. Nine thousand calories but you only live once.

Another of my favorites. Tell me about the café.

It's retro red and white. Jukebox in the corner. Warm and cozy with delicious smells coming from the kitchen. Outside the window, the snow is falling. Big, fat flakes that float down slowly and land with elegance. What's it like where you are tonight?

She watched the three bubbles bouncing on her screen. Then they disappeared. Glancing up, she smiled as the waitress set her dinner on the table. "That looks so good."

"Can I get you anything else?"

"No thank you." She glanced at her phone. Still no response. Maybe he thought her question was too personal, like she was trying to find out where he lived. The bubbles appeared on her screen again, then her phone buzzed.

Sorry. I had to go look out the window. Yes, it's snowing here.

Looks kind of magical. From where I'm sitting, I can see the big tree the town decorates for Christmas. The lights are glowing through the snow. That probably sounds corny, but it really looks beautiful.

Not corny at all. Just wishing I could see what you're seeing.

Her heart did a stupid little pitty-pat. This was getting out of hand. Stupid, stupid, stupid. Time to change from a romantic subject to everyday life. A guy called me nuts today.

She'd opened herself up to anything with that comment. He was probably asking himself why he was texting with a crazy woman. The bubbles on her screen bounced again.

Want me to beat him up for you?

No! Yes. Would you?

Shoot! Would he ask where she lived? Was she ready to reveal?

Actually, no, she quickly texted again. I'm a big girl. Besides, he bought me caramel corn beforehand and it was really good, so I'll suck it up. He's probably right. I can be a little nutty at times. Not that I'm crazy, but I jumped to a lot of conclusions where he was concerned, which wasn't very fair. I should probably apologize, but he's just so irritating. If I say I'm sorry, he'll gloat. For days. See? There I go jumping to conclusions again. I don't even know him and I'm judging.

As soon as she hit *Send*, she regretted it. *Oh my gosh, stop texting! This guy will think you're a nutcase too!* Wow. Sorry for dumping.

Maybe the guy's not as bad as you think.

Most likely he's a nice guy. I mean his mom is really sweet, so he must have some good qualities. We just got off on the wrong foot.

Eat your dinner while it's hot. Talk—text again soon.

Have a nice night.

~

Kevin set his phone down and looked out the front window. Go or not? Because he knew where she was.

Have I lost my mind? She's a nut.

He stuffed his phone into his pocket, grabbed his coat, and headed out into the snow.

He'd come home after his talk with his mom and Murray, found *You've Got Mail* on Demand, and watched Meg Ryan and Tom Hanks make a go of a relationship that grew from nothing but e-mails. As the credits rolled, he decided, come what may, he'd get to know Blue-eyes by texts. He didn't expect a romantic ending like the movie, but maybe they could be friends.

Whipping into a parking spot a few doors from Noelle's Café, he could see her through the window. He put his game face on and walked inside. A waitress he'd known since they were both in elementary school looked up and smiled. "Hey, Kev. You can sit anywhere."

He headed for Ronnie's table. Her attention was turned toward the square outside, so he slipped into the other side of her booth. "Mind if I join you?"

She startled at his voice. More emotions than he could count crossed her face before a tiny smile appeared. "Looks like you already have."

"No one likes to eat alone."

Her smile grew. "You're right."

"Wait, what? Let me get my phone out. I'm pretty sure I have a recorder on it. Can you repeat those words?"

She leaned forward, resting her hands on the table, enunciating carefully. "You're right."

He placed his hands together as if in prayer and looked up at the ceiling. "Thank you," he stage-whispered.

She rolled her eyes.

He pulled her plate toward him. "What's for dinner?"

"Hamburger and fries."

"You didn't finish, young lady," he said, pointing to her half-eaten burger.

She sat back and put a hand on her stomach. "I'm way too full."

"Too full for dessert?" he asked before popping one of her fries into his mouth.

Her blue eyes flashed with a mischievous light. "Dessert?"

"Noelle's serves the best pie in the area."

Ronnie glanced toward the counter as if she didn't believe him. "I really am full."

He turned in his seat. "Lisa, do you have any mixed berry pie left?"

"We do."

"One slice, warmed, à la mode, and two spoons, please."

"Coming right up."

"You know her?" Ronnie asked.

"Little sister of a friend." He popped another fry into his mouth. He'd eaten, but wanted something to keep his hands busy, because—for some reason—he was nervous. "So what brings you out on this snowy night?"

"My basement apartment seemed a little dreary tonight. How about you?"

"I couldn't stop thinking about"—*you*—"Noelle's pies."

"Sweet tooth?"

"Absolutely. You?" he asked.

"Voracious, thus my wolfing down half that caramel corn earlier." She flashed a sly smile. "Does Eden Falls have a gym?"

"We do. Have you met Rowdy yet?"

"On my unfortunate night of assuming."

He nodded, remembering she'd been in Rowdy's bar with Jolie and a bunch of her friends, remembered how annoyed she'd been when he took some of their nachos. "His parents own Get Fit."

"Good to know. I'll have to look into getting a membership."

Lisa delivered a nice-sized piece of pie with vanilla ice cream melting around the sides of the bowl. "Thanks."

"Enjoy."

He gave her a spoon. "Dig in."

She pressed her lips together and narrowed her eyes like she might say no, but took the spoon from him and scooped out a bite. Closing her lips around the spoon and shutting her eyes at the same time, she moaned. "That is so good."

"The best." He took a bite and let the flavors burst over his own taste buds. Tart and sweet, just the way he liked his pie. And his women. Sweet with a little kick. Ronnie was a little like that, although maybe a little heavier on the kick than he was used to.

Ronnie dipped her spoon in for another bite. "Actually, I'm glad you came in."

He glanced up in surprise. "Really?" he asked, barely reining in his sarcasm.

"Yes. I want to apologize for accusing you of manhandling that bird lady. What's her name?"

"Rita Reynolds."

"Right. So, I'm sorry. I was quick to jump to conclusions, which reminds me of my mother. She does that a lot."

"Apology accepted," he said with a nod.

She gave a quick shrug. "I guess we all turn into our parents whether we want to or not."

"Possibly." A few years earlier, his brother Nate had been so worried he'd inherited his father's tendency to desert his family that he almost lost Jolie. No, Kevin would never turn into a person like his father, but he wouldn't mind inheriting a few of his mom's saintly qualities.

He pushed the bowl of dessert toward her.

"One more bite, then I'm done. I'll have to waddle home as it is."

With closed-eyes reverence, she relished her last taste of pie and ice cream, making him chuckle.

"What? It's way too good. Next time I come in I'll get dessert first. Then dinner if there's any room left."

"A girl after my own heart."

The tiniest bit of pink touched her cheeks, or was that his imagination?

She picked up her check and glanced at her phone.

"Expecting a call?"

"No." She shifted in her seat.

Before he stuck the last bite of dessert in his mouth, he asked, "Did you leave a boyfriend back in Spokane?"

"No."

Good. He swiped the check from her hand and grabbed his coat. "Dinner's on me. Consider it a welcome to Eden Falls."

"You don't have to do that," she said while he scooted out of the booth and headed for the register.

She met him there, pulling on her hat and unhooking her coat from the coatrack.

"You two have a good night," Lisa said.

"Oh, we're not—"

"Thanks, Lisa," Kevin said, interrupting Ronnie's protest.

On the sidewalk, he turned to her. "Did you say you walked here?"

"I did."

"Want a ride home?"

"No, I think I'll walk off some of that dessert. Thank you, though, and thanks for buying my dinner. I'll have to work my way through more Washington small towns. It's got me a bouquet, a loaf of bread, caramel corn, and now a dinner."

Eden Falls folks were usually pretty welcoming. He was glad he was included in a couple of the welcome gifts.

He pointed to Town Square. "I'll walk with you."

"You don't have to do that."

"Come on. I want to give you a history lesson about the town's Christmas tree."

They crossed the street and stopped next to the huge pine decorated with colorful lights. "This isn't the original. The first Christmas tree was planted by one of the founding fathers, and it grew to be bigger than this one. About two years ago a group of kids set it on fire."

"Really?"

He nodded.

"Was it an accident?"

"Sadly, no. The kids were from Harrisville, and they set several fires in the area. They even tried to burn down Noelle's Café. Luckily a heavy snow put that fire out."

"Wow. Were they caught?"

"By Rowdy. One night last summer, when he was leaving his bar, he went to check out a strange noise and caught three of the four kids behind The Fly Shop," Kevin said, pointing in that direction. "JT caught the fourth kid trying to get out of town."

"JT?"

"He's the police chief and Alex's brother."

"I haven't met him yet."

Ronnie looked back at the Christmas tree, the lights reflected in her eyes, then at him. "I noticed the charred mountainside just south of town when I came to Eden Falls for my job interview. Were they responsible?"

"Actually, yes. Another kid in their little gang started that fire last summer. Stella almost lost her life that day."

She turned to him, her eyes wide. "She was up there?"

"Rowdy had a house up there, and she'd gone up to walk his dog. The fire climbed the mountain so fast she couldn't get out in time. If Rowdy's dog hadn't led her to a cave…"

"That's crazy scary."

Everyone had been on alert that day. A simple shift in the wind and the whole town could have vanished. "Only a few homes were lost. The fire went over the ridge and firefighters were able to put it out."

"Life can change in a second, can't it?" she said, looking at him.

Kevin realized there was no fighting his attraction to her. He wanted to reach out and touch her, touch her hair, her face. Instead, he buried his hands deeper in his coat pockets.

"Thanks for the history lesson." She smiled. "I better get home before Mrs. O'Malley starts to worry."

"Sure you wouldn't like a ride?"

"No," she said backing away from him. "I only live a couple of blocks away."

He kept watch until she disappeared into the night.

CHAPTER 7

Three days had passed, and Ronnie still hadn't heard from Mystery Man. No call, no text.

She'd considered calling him. She wasn't opposed to taking the lead, but doing so would change the dynamic of their...a word to describe their electronic correspondence didn't pop into her mind. If she mentioned meeting a guy through texts to her parents, they'd both have a fit. Her friends, on the other hand, would consider their nonmeeting conventional, maybe even romantic. She didn't know what to think of it yet.

She knew many people started out with online relationships before ever meeting. She also knew this guy might live on the other side of the country. He hadn't had an identifiable accent, but that didn't mean anything. He could be three times her age, but she couldn't tell from their few brief conversations.

"Ronnie, can you summarize the deposition you sat in on yesterday? I'll need it before tomorrow. Just bullet point the main argument between the clients," Owen said, startling her out of her daydream.

"Sure." She took the digital recorder he handed her.

Owen straightened his tie before shrugging into his overcoat. "I have to run to Harrisville for a lunch meeting. I probably won't be back for the rest of the day."

"I'll e-mail this summary as soon as I finish."

She waved him out the door, glad for something to keep her mind busy. Owen was assigning her more and more responsibilities, which she loved. Her last boss had treated her as if her degree meant nothing. Attaching earbuds to the dictating recorder blocked out the cheery Christmas music playing from a speaker in the reception area, but still enabled her to hear the phone. Owen said the right music calmed people, and she agreed. But most of Owen's clients seemed to know him and were already at ease when they came into the office.

Snow was falling outside again. Though she loved seeing the fat flakes falling just past the parlor window, Eden Falls would be buried if it didn't let up soon.

She popped the earbuds in and got to work, losing track of time until the office grew dark. After finishing the summary, she e-mailed the document to Owen and closed down her computer. Only then did she remove her earbuds and check her phone for the zillionth time. Still nothing. Ronnie was angry at herself for feeling so disappointed, mad that she placed so much hope on a silly wrong number call.

She went through the office, making sure the lights were out and the back door locked, before turning out the Christmas tree lights. Just as she pulled her purse out of her desk drawer, the front door opened and Kevin stepped inside. She tried to wipe the smile off her face without success. As often as she'd looked at her phone, thoughts of Kevin ran through her mind as well. Fighting those thoughts was a waste of time.

"Hi."

"Hi. Owen isn't here," she said, though—somehow—she knew he wasn't here to see Owen, but she couldn't think of anything else to say.

"I'm not here to see Owen."

"Oh."

"I was wondering if you'd like to go to a Christmas party on Friday?"

"W-with you?" she stuttered.

He was bold enough to nod with confidence before closing the distance between them, until they were standing toe to toe.

"Oh, uh, sure." They hadn't exactly gotten along at first, but she had to admit she'd enjoyed his company on Saturday. "Do I need to bring anything?"

"A wrapped white elephant present. I'll pick you up at seven." He started backing toward the door.

"Do you know where I live?"

"Everyone in town knows where you live."

Right. The small-town gossip she'd been warned about by Alex and her friends.

He flashed a smile and disappeared through the door as suddenly as he'd appeared.

~

The next day Kevin had his head under the hood of a Honda Odyssey, thinking about Ronnie incessantly. His invitation to attend the Adams's Christmas party with him had been a spur-of-the-moment decision. He'd been driving past Owen's office, saw the light on, and pulled into the parking lot. Until he opened the door and saw her standing there, purse in hand, he'd had no idea what he was going to say.

Their time together at Noelle's Saturday night was fun.

They'd been able to joke around without snarling at each other, and parted amiably. Not quite friends, but communicating better than they had Saturday morning.

Jolie strolled in with a big paper sack and baby Riley, who reached out as soon as she spotted him.

"Hey, pretty girl. Let me wash my hands." He glanced at Jolie. "What you got there?"

"Sub sandwiches for the hungry brothers."

"That's nice of you." He went to the sink and scrubbed with soap left by a sales rep. "Nate just took out a car he fixed to make sure it's running right."

He slipped his grungy coveralls down to his waist and took his adorable niece from Jolie. "Hey, beautiful."

She grinned and a line of drool dripped onto her cute reindeer sweater.

"That isn't very ladylike." He yanked a paper towel out of a holder and wiped her face. "Hey, is that a tiny tooth?"

"Two tiny teeth. You're seeing her in a happy moment. She's been miserable trying to cut them."

"Aww, poor baby," he said, cuddling her close.

Jolie rubbed her daughter's back while Riley snuggled under his chin. "When are you going to settle down and have one of these?"

"Have you been talking to my mom?"

"No, just watching you with Riley. You'll be such a great dad."

He weighed his words a split second before he blurted out, "I have a date with someone."

"Really? Who?"

"Ronnie Coleman. Actually, it's not a date. I'm taking her to the Adams's Christmas party."

"That's a date," she sing-songed. "I didn't think you and Ronnie got along very well at Rowdy's last week."

"We got past that."

"Good for you." Jolie studied him for a minute. "She's cute."

Instead of replying, he took Riley's hand and patted it against his own. She giggled. He and his last girlfriend didn't date long before she told him she didn't want kids. He'd always wanted two, three, five—maybe more.

Nate walked into the garage from the office. "Hey, honey," he said, bending to kiss his wife and then he smooched his daughter loudly, which made her giggle again.

Nate and Jolie had started dating when they were sixteen, and married ten years later. Kevin used to tease his brother about not playing the field or sampling others' kisses, but now? Now he was jealous of all the years they'd had together. They'd bought a house and started their family. Nate told him a week ago that he was getting a puppy for Riley for Christmas. He was the epitome of a family man.

They went into the office and sat to eat the sandwiches Jolie brought. Or rather Kevin played with his sweet niece while his brother and sister-in-law ate their lunch.

~

A woman entered Owen's office. She waved, but until she took off her knit hat and unwound her scarf, Ronnie didn't recognize Stella.

"I came with an apology and an invitation," she said, leaning against Ronnie's desk.

"Apology for what?"

"For not inviting you to my parents' Christmas party sooner. It's on Friday at seven."

"I actually have a date that night."

"Bring him with you."

Ronnie laughed. "He's already bringing me to the party."

She could see the sudden flare of interest in Stella's eyes.

She scooted onto the corner of Ronnie's desk. "Really? Who is this date with?"

What would it hurt to tell? Everyone would know as soon as they walked into the party anyway. "Kevin Klein."

Stella frowned. "After what happened at Rowdy's? I thought you two didn't like each other."

Ronnie lifted a shoulder. "We have our differences."

"Rowdy and I sure had our differences." Her eyebrows bounced playfully. "Funny how those differences disappeared after a great kiss."

Being new in town, Ronnie couldn't help wondering about the different couples and their stories. She knew Stella taught the second grade and Rowdy owned a bar and grill. How did they work around their schedules? "What happened?"

Stella went all googly-eyed. "He kissed me at Carolyn and JT's wedding reception under a sky full of stars. How I managed to walk back to the reception on knees of jelly, I'll never know."

Ronnie sat on her desk next to Stella. "Romantic."

"Very. And embarrassing. Rowdy and I had been friends forever, and I'd never thought of him as anything beyond that. To make matters worse, Beam caught us."

"Beam?"

"Rowdy's brother and Misty's husband. Luckily, he kept the news to himself, which gave Rowdy and me time to work things out. I'd just found out the week before that my boyfriend of two years was married. With three kids."

"Wow, and I thought my life was complicated. Sounds like small-town life can be as exciting as living in a big city."

"Probably more so," Stella said, rolling her eyes dramatically. "News travels fast, and no secret is safe." She glanced around the law firm's reception area. "How do you like the new job?"

"Love it."

"And Eden Falls? Are you settling in okay?"

"I love it here so far."

"Good." Stella jumped off the desk and tugged her knit hat back into place. "I have to get back to school. My second graders will be out of their art class in a few minutes. I'll see you tomorrow night."

Ronnie waved her out the door. Small-town people talked, and likely they were fiercely loyal to their own. She started to worry about her acceptance of Kevin's invitation. What would happen if she and Kevin decided they weren't really compatible? She only knew a few details about him.

She'd entered the dating waters alone, and navigated through the turbulent currents without an older sibling to talk to, or a younger sibling to compare notes with. As a teenager, she'd vowed if she ever had children, she'd have more than one. People complained about their brothers and sisters all the time, but she'd give anything to have one, even if only to deflect her parents' attention once in a while. She would have loved that break growing up.

At the end of the day she bundled up against the cold and drove to the only Christmas tree lot in town. Before she got out of the car, her phone pinged with a text message.

How was your day?

Mystery Guy. She'd been anxiously waiting to hear from him—that is, until Kevin asked her out. Suddenly the lines became blurred. She wasn't sure how to answer. Did she tell him she had a date? Or keep that information to herself?

Dishonesty bugged her, even if she didn't know the guy, other than the little she'd learned from a few texts.

Though she hadn't made a commitment to either one, she wasn't a two-guys-at-the-same-time kind of girl. Kevin lived in Eden Falls. Mystery Guy could live anywhere. Kevin co-owned a prosperous auto shop. She didn't know what mystery guy did for a living, or if he even had a job. Kevin was irritating but could also be sweet. Without meeting the guy on her phone, she knew absolutely nothing about him. They'd only talked twice. She wasn't sure she'd recognize his voice even if he called rather than texted. And *why* all the texting? You could only assume inflection in a text, which was sometimes taken wrong. You couldn't hear cadence or tone. LOL or a laughing emoji weren't the same as hearing the sound of delight, anger, surprise, or fear.

My day was good. I can't really text now. I just stopped to get a Christmas tree.

Our timing always seems to be off.

Maybe that was a sign. She texted back, Karma?

Coincidence or divine decree. I don't really believe in karma.

She didn't either, but neither did she believe in divine decree. There is nothing divine about you calling the wrong number.

I called the right number. You answered.

His quick comeback made her smile.

I'll let you go. Pick out a nice-smelling tree.

I will. Bye Mystery Man.

Bye Anonymous Woman.

*K*evin raced to pull on his coat and hat. There was only one Christmas tree lot in Eden Falls. If he hurried, he could get there before she finished.

Max stepped into the office, wiping his hands on a rag. "Mrs. Laske's car is finished. Can you—?"

"Gotta go. I'll see you tomorrow."

"Wait—"

Kevin was out the door before Max could stop him.

Jumping into his truck, he only went five miles over the speed limit to get to the other side of town. He spotted her car, still in the parking lot, when he turned in.

While he was walking among the trees, snow started falling again. Light flakes drifted down, like little white fairies dancing among the pine branches. He wove his way along the aisles, greeting several people he knew.

"Looking for a tree?"

He dropped his head and smiled. She'd found him. He turned. "Yes. You?"

She lifted her shoulders up around her ears. "I have to admit this is a first for me. I've never bought a Christmas tree before."

If he was truthful, he'd admit it was his first time too. He'd helped his mom every year before Murray came into their lives, but not very many times since, and never for himself. "What size are you looking for?"

Stepping close enough that he caught a breath of her perfume, she looked up at him. "How tall are you?"

Under the lights of the tree lot, he could see the navy rim around the outside of her sparkling blue eyes. "Six two."

"That's how tall I want my tree, but it has to be skinny."

He chuckled. "Are you saying I'm fat?"

"No," she laughed, putting a hand on his chest and just as quickly jerking it back when he looked down. "I only have one spot where a tree will fit, and it's a narrow space."

"So, we're looking for tall and skinny."

She led him through the pines, the spicy fragrance heavy in the air. He spotted a thin tree and examined the ticket. "What about this balsam?"

Lifting brows, she looked from the tree to him. "Nice, but too fat."

"You could cut off the back branches if it's going to be against the wall."

She shook her head with crinkled nose. "Still too wide.

"Okay." He pointed to another tree not far away. "How about that one?"

Circling the tree, she shook her head. "The back is naked."

"Naked?" He turned the tree to see several missing branches. "That's the side that will go against the wall."

"I want a whole tree."

Her logic didn't make sense to him, but it was her tree.

They looked at several more pines before her eyes lit up. "This is the one." She walked around the tall, skinny spruce, her face glowing with happiness. "It's perfect."

He stifled a laugh. The tree was the saddest-looking one in the lot, and she thought it was perfect. "To each their own."

"So cliché. Despite what you think, I love it."

He lifted his hands in surrender. "Hey, it's your tree. If you think it's perfect, that's all that matters."

She flipped the ticket over. "The price is within my budget."

"You go pay the man and I'll load it into my truck."

"No need. The tree will fit on the top of my car."

"Why tie the tree up and risk losing it halfway home when we can just put it in the back of my truck?"

She studied him for a long moment. "What about you?"

"What about me?"

"Your tree? Didn't you come here to buy one too?"

Oh, right. His reason for being here.

He and Max had never had a tree in their apartment. The only spot he could think to put one was the tall sill of the bay window in their living room. He'd have to buy lights and ornaments. This "chance" meeting was going to be more expensive than he'd thought. "I need one about this tall," he said, holding his hand at about three feet.

She smiled. "Fat or skinny?"

The sill on the bay window was wide. "Doesn't matter."

Taking his gloved hand in hers, she led him around the trailer Mel Hancock worked and lived out of during the Christmas tree season. "I saw this one when I came in and thought it was so cute."

The tree was a fat little fir that would hold a thousand lights. "Just what every man wants, a cute tree."

"You can make it manly. Hang some wrenches and screwdrivers from the branches," she said with a twinkle in her eye.

He nodded and pulled the ticket off a branch. "Sold."

They loaded the trees in the back of his truck, then he opened the door of her car so she could slide behind the wheel. "I'll follow you."

CHAPTER 8

Kevin pulled into Mrs. O'Malley's driveway and parked behind her car. Ronnie watched from her rearview mirror while he climbed out of his truck before she got out.

Despite their differences, she'd had fun with him tonight. A lot of fun. And they hadn't disagreed once.

He lowered the tailgate of his truck and pulled the pine out until she was able to take the top while he carried the trunk. The tree was more awkward than she expected, and she was grateful for the help.

"I know this sounds dumb, but I'm really excited to have a tree this year." To be totally honest with herself, she was kind of excited about Kevin, too.

He chuckled.

She liked that he laughed often.

Since the tree was so skinny, it fit through the door easily. Once inside, she hurried into the bedroom to get the tree stand she'd bought. "Do you have any plans?"

"You mean right now?"

She nodded. "If you'll help me get the tree upright, I'll feed you."

"Yeah?" he asked, surprise in his voice. "What are you going to feed me?"

"Homemade chicken noodle soup and some of your mom's bread."

"Perfect tree-decorating food."

His answer gave her a tingly surprise in the pit of her stomach. She'd thought about asking, but figured a mechanic was not the kind of guy who'd want to decorate for Christmas.

They got the tree standing straight while the soup warmed and the bread thawed.

"Let me get dinner dished."

"If you'll tell me where everything is, I'll set the table."

"You set tables?"

He lifted a brow. "I could take offense at that question. I'm not a Neanderthal."

"I'm sorry, I just—"

"You met my mom. Do you really think she wouldn't have taught her sons how to make beds, do laundry, *and* set tables? Where are the bowls?"

She pointed to one of three small cupboards. The kitchen in her apartment was tiny, with hardly any storage space. "The silverware is in the top drawer and the napkins are already on the table."

After his first bite, he smiled. "This is really good."

"Thank you."

While they ate, he told her stories of his childhood. Even though his younger years were hard after his father left, he and his brothers had made the best of life with a loving mother's help. He told her about the boys sharing rooms in their two-bedroom apartment, while their mom slept on the sofa. How he and Max had played games with the younger boys while their mom worked two jobs and sometimes three to make ends meet.

"I'm sorry."

He shrugged in a what-you-gonna-do way. "Times were hard, but we made it through okay. My mom is happily remarried. My stepdad saved us, raised us as his own."

She passed him the plate with slices of bread. "I can tell by the way you talk that you really like your stepdad."

"Love him. He's a great man. Would we have survived without him? Sure. But he changed our lives, changed my mom's life. She was able to quit working and be a mom."

"Do you ever see your dad?"

Kevin buttered a second piece of bread. "He calls when he needs money."

"Does he live close by?" She set the plate on the table and took a piece for herself.

"He moves around a lot."

She imagined it would hurt to have your father leave, and that it was probably difficult to talk about it. She shouldn't have been so inquisitive.

"Tell me about your childhood," he said after another bite of soup. "Was it hard being an only child?"

"Not hard, just lonely sometimes. I always wanted a brother or sister. I have great parents, but they can be a little…"

"Overbearing?"

"*Attentive* is a better description. Because I am an only child, they tend to be overprotective, focusing all their energy and attention on me. They're both scientists and wanted me to follow in their footsteps, but I didn't want anything to do with science. So what's the next best thing? Marry her off to a scientist. Why are you laughing?"

"I'm just trying to picture you as a coddled teen, which I can't. You're so…"

"Bossy?"

"I was going to say assertive, but okay."

Ronnie never thought of herself as assertive. She was more an introvert than outgoing, but she was trying to break through her self-imposed barriers. Standing, she cleared her bowl. "Would you like more soup?"

"No, thank you. That was really good." He cleared the rest of the table. "Where do you store your Christmas decorations?"

"I always went home for the holidays, so I've never decorated my own place before. I only have the few things I've bought since I moved here." She darted into the bedroom where she'd shoved a couple of bags into her closet.

He took them from her when she came back into the living room. "I think you're going to have to do some more shopping. These ornaments will only cover the top fourth of your tree."

"I don't mind shopping." She flashed a smile. "As you pointed out at the bazaar."

"I did, didn't I?"

She shrugged. "I'll start at the top and work my way down."

"Want some help with your lights?" he asked, taking several boxes from a bag. "I think you have enough to cover the tree."

While she took the lights out of the boxes, he strung them around the tree, careful to hit every branch. She was touched by the way he took such care with a tree for someone he didn't know very well.

"How were you going to decorate a tree as tall as I am without a ladder?"

"I'm pretty sure Mrs. O'Malley has a stepladder I could borrow in the garage."

When the lights were on, he picked up a hand-painted ornament. "Where do you want this?"

She spent the next fifteen minutes directing him where to hang the few ornaments she'd bought at the church bazaar.

"Last one," he said, pulling out a ball of greenery Alex had given her when she went into Pretty Posies. "Except you can't stand under the mistletoe if you hang it on the tree."

"That's mistletoe?"

Kevin smiled. "You're supposed to hang it in a doorway and, with every kiss, a berry is removed."

"I don't see any berries being removed in my apartment. You're the first visitor I've had."

One side of his mouth quirked as he held the mistletoe over her head. "We could remove a berry right now."

She looked up at the green leaves and white berries as her pulse picked up speed. "We don't know each other very well."

"It's just a kiss. Not a marriage proposal."

She looked into his mischievous eyes and shrugged a shoulder. "True. It's just a kiss."

Without touching her with his hands, he bent and pressed his lips to hers. A sweet tingle started at the back of her neck and moved down her spine. The heat of attraction made her breath catch in her throat. She'd always liked first kisses, so full of possibilities.

Slowly she opened her eyes and found him staring at her, his mischievous expression gone. When he swallowed, his Adam's apple bobbed.

He cleared his throat. "See? A simple kiss."

"Yep." Her heart sped up again when his gaze dropped to her mouth. Instead of taking the mistletoe from him when he offered it, she plucked a berry off and dropped it into a heart-shaped bowl on her coffee table.

"I'd better go. I have to get my own tree into water."

"Thank you for your help," she said, cradling the mistletoe in a hand.

"Thank you for dinner. The soup was delicious."

From the door, she watched him disappear around the house into the darkness, the snow still gently falling.

Closing the door, she turned out the lights, enjoying the sparkling colors on her tree and the expanding emotions filling her heart, before she bundled up to shovel away the snow.

Kevin drove home in a daze. The kiss he'd shared with Ronnie wasn't just a kiss. At least to him. He'd felt like that after a kiss before, but not for a very, *very* long time. And that encounter hadn't ended well. Unlike half the guys who grew up in Eden Falls, he had dated locally. Nothing ever developed until he met Faith Dunning. They'd been hot and heavy for a year, but just as quickly as their love began, it fizzled like a drop of water on a hot skillet.

He could never put his finger on the reason why, other than they'd started out physical with no underlying substance. They still ran into each other once in a while, suffered through awkward conversations when they had to, but both would rather avoid meeting at all. She'd since married, and he hoped she was happy. He felt no animosity—and hoped she didn't either—but he wasn't anxious for a repeat of history. So his brief moment with Ronnie had left him wanting more and ready to run in the opposite direction at the same time.

By the time he parked in front of his apartment, he couldn't remember even turning into his complex. He put the truck into park as his mind traveled back to his and

Ronnie's evening together. The undercurrent of tension that had shadowed them until now seemed to have evaporated like an early morning mist.

Grabbing his phone from the console, he considered texting that something had come up on Friday and he couldn't make the party after all, which was ridiculous. He hadn't missed the Adams's Christmas party since he was a little kid. And if he texted Ronnie about the party, she'd know he was the one who'd called the wrong number.

Instead, he went inside and waited a long hour—fighting a good fight against himself. Finally he texted, How did your Christmas tree hunt go?

It took her several minutes to reply. Dancing bubbles appeared, then stopped, then reappeared several times. He wondered what was going through her mind.

Good. The tree is up.

Great. How does it look?

Naked. I need more decorations.

'Tis the season.

The bubbles began to bounce immediately after his text. Again, he watched them stop and start several times before her text came through.

I met someone.

He studied her message for a long moment, then smiled. I'm certainly not one to stand in the way of love.

It's not love. We haven't even been on a date, but I'd like to see if anything develops. I don't feel comfortable texting you and seeing—maybe seeing—someone else. I'm sorry.

Nothing to be sorry for. This has been fun while it lasted, he texted back. Who knows? Maybe it will turn into love. Goodbye, Sexy Voice.

Have a wonderful holiday season, Mystery Man.

He glanced in his rearview mirror and caught his stupidly happy reflection grinning back at him.

~

*R*onnie stared at the message he'd sent, wishing her luck. Whether anything developed between Kevin and her—even if their date went wrong on Friday night and she never saw him again—she'd made the right choice by telling Mystery Man she was seeing someone.

Picking up the mistletoe that she'd set on the table when she went outdoors to shovel, she touched the fingertips of her other hand to her lips. She hadn't been kissed in a while. Though it was just a simple meeting of their lips, she'd felt his breath on her face like a stroke of a feather. The impact left her wanting more.

Turning off the overhead switch, she let the tree lights send their many colors around the room. As a child she would put her favorite ornament low on a branch at the back of the tree, then she'd lie on her back and watch how the light would reflect off the glass. Sometimes she saw her own reflection in the bulbs. Other times she stared through the branches and inhaled the scent of pine.

Her phone rang through the quiet, startling her. Her mom's face lit her cell screen. "Hi, Mom."

"How are you, sweetheart?"

"I'm good and work is good."

"That's wonderful."

Ronnie wrapped a throw around herself and sat on the sofa. "I like this town."

"It's awfully small. Have you met anyone?"

Where should she start? "I was invited out for appetizers and drinks with five other women about my age. I've met a café owner and the librarian. I'm invited to a Christmas party this Friday." She left out the date part. Her mom would want to know what Kevin did for a living and would not be impressed to hear he was a mechanic, whether or not he owned his own shop.

~

The next day, Max walked into the shop office and shrugged out of his coat. "Why do we have a Christmas tree in our apartment?"

"I bought it on a whim."

"Do we even have decorations?"

"Ma has given us each an ornament every year since we were born. Between us, that's sixty-six ornaments."

Max laughed. "You kept those?"

"Clearly you didn't."

"I might have a couple. I'll have to look."

Kevin shook his head. Responsibility had never been one of Max's strengths, except when it came to cars. He'd have to stop by the store for a couple of strings of lights. It wouldn't take many to brighten that little tree.

"Where were you last night?" Max asked, coming around the desk. "Ma sent some chili over."

Kevin wasn't ready to share that he'd been with Ronnie. He wanted to keep it to himself for a while longer. People in town would find out soon enough when they saw them together this Friday. "I was buying a tree."

"I'm pretty sure the tree lot isn't open after eight."

"Since Mel stays in his trailer on the lot, he can stay open as late as he wants. How's the online dating going?" he asked, ready to divert the conversation.

"Good. I think this girl might be the one."

"What? You've gone out with her two times!"

"Love at first sight."

The UPS truck stopped in front of the shop, and Kevin rounded the desk to hold the door open for their delivery.

"You actually think you're in love with someone you've seen twice?"

"It can happen. Ma only dated Murray for three months before they got married."

"Three months is not the same as seeing someone two times, Max. And Ma and Murray were a lot older than you."

"Hey, Duane," Max said when the UPS driver wheeled a dolly into the reception area.

"Hey, guys. You want this stuff in here or the garage?"

Max pushed open the garage door. "Just drop the boxes in the corner."

While Max and Duane talked engines, Kevin stayed in the shop. He'd fallen for Faith fast and hard, but wondered now if it was ever love. If it had been love, they would have experienced sadness or heartache when they broke up. Instead he felt nothing at all. One day they were together, the next day they weren't.

Here he was chiding Max about falling too fast. Maybe he should take a step back and examine his own feelings. What he was experiencing with Ronnie was fresh and growing fast, unlike anything he'd ever felt before. The thought of her was enough to tighten his stomach muscles and set his heart pounding erratically. Was this love?

CHAPTER 9

The time on Friday moved at a snail's pace. On her lunch hour, Ronnie rushed to a couple of the gift shops around the square.

Alex carried fun decorations from local artisans at Pretty Posies, so Ronnie picked up several cute ornaments there, too. Every time she went in, she expected to hear that Alex had given birth to her baby and, every time, Alex greeted her with her radiant smile. She made pregnancy seem like the most wondrous gift on earth. Maybe it was.

Ronnie had never really thought about having children, other than if she did, she'd want more than one. Her mom and dad were able to have more, but chose not to. A child's school schedule and ballet lessons interfered with people as career-minded as her parents. They worked for a clinical research company and were always searching for the next greatest medication. Though they'd made more than enough time for her, she was aware she never had one hundred percent of their attention.

Her workload was winding down due to the holidays. When she got back to the office, Owen told her to take the rest of the day off, so she drove to Harrisville, a much larger town, to purchase Christmas gifts for her parents, who were hard to buy for. They had plenty of money and bought what they needed at the time. Still, she found a pretty sweater for her mom and a nice tie for her dad. She'd add a few gift certificates for books. Both read a lot at work but enjoyed reading for pleasure as well.

A picture frame made of different sizes of wrenches caught her eye. On a whim, she bought it. She and Kevin probably wouldn't exchange gifts, but it would be better to be prepared than not. After she took the bag from the cashier, though, she felt silly. For all she knew tonight could be her first and last date with Kevin. She was also surprised that she was letting herself think long-term with a guy she couldn't stand a week ago.

On her way home, she drove past Klein's Auto Shop. Kevin was in the reception area, sweeping or mopping.

A drive-by stalker. You are pathetic, girl.

At home, Ronnie pulled out several outfits, wishing she'd bought something new for tonight. She wasn't sure what to wear since this was her first Christmas party in Eden Falls. After changing more times than she'd ever admit, she finally decided on a red sweater dress and knee-high boots with heels. Festive yet informal, but not so casual that she'd look out of place.

Kevin was right on time.

She opened the door, hoping they wouldn't feel uncomfortable around each other. His grin put her at ease immediately. "Come in," she said, opening the door wider.

She wasn't nervous until he looked at her mouth, reminding her of their kiss. A quick moment in time. Sweet. Sexy. He'd given her a taste of what could be.

He stepped inside and stopped next to her tree. "You bought more decorations."

"It doesn't look so naked now."

She wished she could read his expression when he looked at her. His smile was gone, but his eyes twinkled. Something a little magical. He kept a tiny bit to himself. Her parents always told her she wore her feelings on her sleeve. She didn't know how to hide the emotions she felt when Kevin was near. Really didn't see any need to. "What are you thinking?"

He shook his head, the corners of his mouth twitching.

She noticed he was wearing jeans and a button-down shirt and she looked down at her dress. "I wasn't sure what to wear."

"You look pretty perfect."

Though she knew he just meant she was dressed okay for the party, his comment made her smile.

"Are you ready to go?"

When she picked up her coat from the sofa, he took it from her and held it out. She met his gaze.

"My mother taught me right," he said. "You met her. I don't want her coming after me for not holding your coat or a door."

Ronnie slipped her arms in and they stepped outside, locking the door behind them. True to his word, he opened the truck door and helped her up.

They drove across town making small talk about their day. Simple, comfortable. She hoped she'd know people at the party. She imagined Stella's friends would be there, along with their husbands. She also hoped Kevin wouldn't abandon her to fend for herself.

"The Adams family have lived in Eden Falls forever. They have five daughters. Three—Phoebe, Stella, and Izzy—live in town."

"Hey, your mom has five boys and they have five girls. Have you ever thought..." Even as she made the suggestion, a little sluice of jealousy made its way through her.

"There were a few crossovers. Stella and Max might have dated in high school."

She remembered the comments exchanged between the two at Rowdy's. "I think you're right."

"And my little brother Cam and Adelaide Adams dated before they went away to college."

Tonight would be helpful. She was always better with names once she put them with faces.

Kevin turned down a street lined with cars. "Are all these people at the party?"

"Probably. I can drop you off and find a place to park."

"I can walk."

"Your heels—"

"I'll be fine if I can hold onto your arm."

He flashed a smile at her that didn't go away when he looked back at the road.

They didn't have to drive too far before he found a spot, and when they got out, he reached into the backseat and pulled out a covered bowl, while she carried the two wrapped white elephant presents.

"Why didn't you tell me we were supposed to bring food, too?"

"You're my guest. Trust me, I brought plenty." He crooked his elbow, and she stacked one present on the other and took his arm. The sidewalks were cleared, but she didn't let go.

He opened the door without ringing the bell, and they entered a house teeming with people. Kevin nodded toward a tree. "We can put the presents there."

She shrugged out of her coat, then held the bowl while he did the same. He took both coats into an office next to the front door and stacked them on top of what looked like a hundred others, then introduced her as they moved through the living room to the kitchen where he put the bowl on a counter overflowing with food.

"Hi, Ronnie," Carolyn said, sidling up beside her. "Did you hear Alex delivered a baby boy about an hour ago?"

"What? I just saw her at Pretty Posies on my lunch hour."

Carolyn introduced her tall, handsome husband, JT— Chief of Police of Eden Falls.

Next she met Kevin's stepdad and talked with his mom, who made it clear she was glad they'd come together. Kevin introduced her to the host and hostess of the party, Stella's parents, and they seemed to be as crazy fun as Stella was.

Next she and Kevin filled their plates with yummy foods —finger sandwiches, a delicious crab dip, and divine desserts. Ronnie had never been to a party like this. The really nice part was everyone knew everyone else. She was the odd one out, but didn't feel like it. People she didn't know came up and introduced themselves, because everyone had heard about Owen's new employee.

She finally got to meet Kevin's brother Nate, and Stella's older sister, police officer named Phoebe. She talked to Isadora Adams, who was renovating the Victorian next to Owen's office. And the whole time Kevin stayed close by, helping her with a name when she slipped up. He made her feel special in the fact that he didn't leave her alone to go talk to buddies or refill his plate.

*K*evin couldn't remember the last time he'd enjoyed himself so much at one of these parties. Though he kept his hands to himself, he liked having Ronnie close. Touching the small of her back when leading her from one room to another was all he allowed himself. She looked like she was having fun, and seemed to enjoy putting a face to the names she recognized, so he tried to introduce her to as many people as possible without overwhelming her.

Faith was watching him from across the room. Most people were probably shocked to see him here with a date after coming alone for so many years. Yep. His mom and stepdad were also watching, along with Stella and Rowdy. He felt like they were on display, but knew the townsfolk would get their staring over within one night and move on to someone new tomorrow. The next time he and Ronnie went out, people would be used to seeing them together.

Getting ahead of yourself there, Kev. After being on display tonight, she might never want to go out with you again.

She glanced up with big eyes, so blue they stole his breath away. He took her arm, leading her to the doorway that led into the hall. "You look like you could use a break."

Settling against the doorframe, she smiled and shook her head. "Actually, I'm having a really good time."

"Not overwhelmed?"

"Kind of, but in a good way." Her smile was shy, which didn't match the Ronnie he knew. "Everyone is so nice here. Thank you for inviting me."

He leaned against the opposite side of the doorframe. "You're welcome."

Stella moved toward them and nudged him with her elbow. "You are adorable."

"Don't think I've ever been included in a sentence with the word *adorable*," he said. He glanced at Ronnie. "She must be talking about you."

"I was talking about the way you led Ronnie to the only place where my parents hang mistletoe." Stella pointed up. "And there are plenty of berries left."

He glanced up, then looked down to see Ronnie's wide-eyed but interested reaction.

"Most people steer clear of this doorway to avoid public display," Stella teased.

Ronnie flashed another shy smile. "Did you do this on purpose?"

He shook his head. "No, but we might as well take advantage."

He put his finger under Ronnie's chin and bent to kiss her smile away. When he straightened, everyone in the kitchen hooted catcalls and applauded.

~

Monday afternoon, Owen walked into the reception area with another file. "I'm sorry to make you work late tonight, Ronnie. The judge in Harrisville blindsided me with this case."

"I don't mind." Which was true. Owen didn't ask much of her, so she was happy to help.

He smiled, took his glasses off, and polished the lenses with the special cloth he kept in his shirt pocket. "It was good to see you at the party Friday. Looks like you're making friends."

If he hadn't witnessed her and Kevin's kiss, he was sure to have heard about it, but Owen wasn't the type to bring up something that might embarrass her. "I am. It was fun to meet so many people."

He settled his glasses back on his nose. "Are you going home anytime over the holidays?"

"I'll drive over for a day or two."

"Take a couple of extra days. Make it a long weekend."

She'd appreciate the extra time off, but not to spend in Spokane. She had moved in over a weekend and started a new job the very next Monday, so having some time to finish unpacking and organizing her apartment would be welcome. "Maybe.

"Thank you again for working tonight."

"I really don't mind, Owen."

After he went back to his office, she picked up her cell phone to call Kevin. She'd invited him to dinner at her house tonight. Scrolling through her contacts, she realized they hadn't exchanged phone numbers yet. All his invitations had been face-to-face.

She looked up the shop's number and called.

"Klein's Auto Shop. This is Nate."

"Hi, Nate. This is Ronnie. We met at—"

"I remember who you are. Is your car acting up again?"

"No. I was calling to talk to Kevin. Is he in?"

"He had to run to Harrisville for a couple of parts. He should be back in an hour."

She pulled a pad of paper over and grabbed a pen. "Can I get his number?"

"Sure."

Ronnie wrote the numbers down as he rattled them off. "Thanks, Nate."

She saved the number to Klein's Auto Shop in her cell phone—which felt like another step toward a possible relationship—then started to put in the new number, but her phone showed she already had a contact under that number.

Mystery Man.

Wait!

That couldn't be right. Kevin would have—

She looked from the pad of paper to her phone. No mistake. The number was the same. Did Kevin know? She tried to think back. They'd never exchanged numbers, but right after she texted with Mystery Man about the retro café, Kevin had shown up. Then the tree lot.

He knew! So why didn't he tell her?

And when did he discover...?

The church bazaar.

Mystery Man had called and hung up when she answered. Kevin must have recognized her voice and was afraid she'd recognize his.

The rat! He'd been playing her. Deceiving her. For over a week. But why? What had he gained? Other than a few kisses.

Her cheeks heated at the betrayal. Was this some elaborate plan to humiliate her after she'd jumped to so many conclusions?

Did everyone in town know?

The sting of tears embarrassed her, even though no one was around to see. Maybe Eden Falls wasn't such a nice place after all.

CHAPTER 10

Kevin slid behind the wheel of his truck just as his phone pinged a new message.

Sorry can't cook dinner tonight. Have to work.

Disappointment hit him hard. I'm sorry too. How about tomorrow night?

Nope. I'm busy all week.

All week? he texted, then waited for a reply that didn't come. How about Saturday night?

Again, no reply. He set his phone in the console for the drive from Harrisville to Eden Falls, surprised she didn't suggest a time when she might be free. She'd told him Owen was postponing cases until after the first of the year, so her having to work late all week didn't make sense.

Both brothers were waiting when he entered the garage bay by the side door. He set the box with the part on a workbench and turned to them. "What's up?"

Nate pulled a rag from his coveralls back pocket and wiped his hands, brother number three's nervous habit. "Max and I have been talking. Though we carry the basics, the closest auto parts store is in Harrisville—"

"So why aren't we cashing in on those parts?" Max interjected. "We could build onto the other side of the shop and sell parts to people who fix their own cars."

Nate tucked the rag back in his pocket. "Makes sense, don't you think, Kev? We're losing a lot of potential business from people who drive to Harrisville for their parts."

"It makes perfect sense, and I've thought the same thing several times, but building on will mean dipping heavily into our profits. You and Jolie have a house and a baby. And Jolie isn't working."

"I know. We've talked." Nate walked over to the workbench, opened the box, and pulled out one of the parts. "Ronnie is working as a paralegal for Owen. He's hiring a receptionist after the first of the year. He told Jolie at the Adams's party she could come back and work three days a week if she wants the job. Her mom offered to babysit for us."

"And Ma would help," Max was quick to add. "She's always offering to watch Riley."

Nate and Jolie were Kevin's first consideration when thinking about business plans. Though change involved all of them, Nate had the most to lose. "Okay, let's sit down and talk about it," he said, "but Jolie should be in on this conversation."

Nate smiled, reminding Kevin of their dad. Of all the Klein boys, Nate had their biological dad's smile. "You guys come to the house tomorrow night for dinner. We'll weigh the pros and cons."

Kevin unloaded the other parts and stacked them on shelves. "Shouldn't you talk to Jolie first?"

"I already did. Dinner was her suggestion."

And there was that twinge of jealousy again. Of course Nate would have discussed this with Jolie first.

Nate turned to the car he'd been working on. "Oh, I

almost forgot. Ronnie called here looking for you. I gave her your number."

"Yeah, she—" *Oh, crap!* His stomach took a nosedive.

They hadn't exchanged numbers yet. If she kept the number he'd been texting from before, she'd know it matched his cell number.

Great job, Kev.

"What's that look for?" Max asked.

He shook his head. "She texted me as I was leaving the auto parts store."

Stupid. He should have been up front with her as soon as he realized who she was. She probably didn't have to work late, just used that as an excuse to break their date.

Max chuckled. "The two of you seem to be moving fast."

"Fast? How do you figure?"

"She's only been in Eden Falls for two weeks and you're already kissing her in front of the whole town."

"It was one kiss under the mistletoe."

"Ri-i-ight," Max teased.

Kevin went into the office to work some numbers, and all the while thoughts of Ronnie niggled at the back of his mind.

Nate walked in and plopped down in a chair. "What's bugging you?"

For a split second he thought his brother was referring to Ronnie, then realized he was talking business. "I'm just worried about putting you under a financial strain, Nate."

"If Jolie goes back to work, this new venture will pan out."

Kevin picked up a pencil and tapped it on the desk. "Yes, but she likes staying at home with Riley."

"She does, but she also likes working for Owen." Nate leaned forward and rested his elbows on his thighs. "This will get Jolie out of the house a few days a week. It wouldn't be feasible if her mom hadn't offered to help. Now Riley will be around family rather than strangers at a daycare. You know Owen. Being a family man and very involved in his own sons' activities, he'll work around Jolie and Riley's schedule. And I'm sure Ronnie could cover the front desk if Riley is sick or something comes up."

The mention of her name conjured Ronnie front and center again. She'd never told him she was working as a paralegal. She said her job title was executive assistant. Not that a job title mattered to him, but she hadn't revealed everything either.

Now you're being petty.

"This could work, Kev."

"Startup will be expensive, but with a loan we could probably make it work. We could talk to Gunner Stone, see if he'd be willing to be contractor for the addition. He should be finished with the renovations on the Victorian next door to Owen's office after the first of the year." He'd have to write up a business plan for the bank, which he'd done before.

Nate stood and walked to the door of the office. "I have to install that part before I go home. Don't worry about Jolie and me. We can make this work."

Kevin ran numbers until Max came in to say they were closing up. He'd lost track of time making lists and considering details. Tomorrow night, when they sat down to discuss this plan, he wanted to present solid facts rather than "what-ifs" and "maybes."

Max laughed at Kevin's pile of notes. "You always were a geek at heart."

Kind of true. He'd always loved facts and numbers. They spoke the truth, were specific, made sense. "Being precise isn't geeky."

Nate poked his head around the door. "Tomorrow night at six."

Kevin waved. "Yeah. Tell Jolie thanks."

"Will do. See ya in the morning."

"Bye, geek," Max said, and walked out with Nate.

Kevin sat back in his chair and laced his fingers behind his head, thoughts of Ronnie still nagging at him. For the first time since he and Faith drifted apart, he felt like his life was about to change in the most incredible, indescribable way. And he might have ruined everything with a simple act of omission. He wasn't sure how he could fix this, but knew he had to try.

On his way home he drove past Owen's office. The lights were still burning in several rooms, and Ronnie's snow-covered car was in the parking lot, proving she hadn't concocted the story of working late. He pulled in, brushed her car clean, and scraped the windows.

~

*R*onnie got out of her car in front of Alex's house, climbed the front porch steps, and knocked. A boy opened the door and flashed a huge smile. "Hi!"

"Hello. I'm Ronnie Coleman."

The kid's eyes lit with enthusiasm. "Are you here to see my mom and new brother?"

"If your mom is Alex, then yes, I am."

Alex shuffled to the door in a robe, carrying a blue bundle in her arms. "Come in. You caught me in my pajamas."

"I think new moms have earned the right to stay in their pajamas all day if they like," Ronnie said, stepping inside.

Alex touched the boy's shoulder. "This is my son Charlie. And our new addition, Benjamin."

She turned the baby so Ronnie could see the shock of blond hair. Such a contrast to the other boy's black hair and dark eyes. The baby's eyes were scrunched closed and his tiny rosebud mouth worked furiously like he was chewing something. Ronnie was tempted to run her knuckle down the baby's rosy cheek, but didn't.

"Charlie's been a big help since we brought his little brother home."

"Do you like having a brother, Charlie?"

Charlie tipped his hand back and forth. "He cries a lot when I try to hold him."

"I bet that will change when he gets to know you better," Ronnie said. "I brought a chicken pot pie for one of your dinners. You can freeze it or eat it within the next couple of days. Cooking directions are on the top." She'd made it ahead of time, for the dinner she canceled with Kevin. She'd planned to send him home with the leftovers, but now it would be dinner for a new friend and her family.

"That is so kind of you."

A man walked into the room and extended his hand. "Hi, I'm Colton."

Ronnie closed her hanging jaw as she shook the author's hand. She looked at Alex in awe. "You're married to Colton McCreed?"

"Guilty."

"I've read all your books. I had no idea. You live in Eden Falls?"

"Guilty," he said, placing a hand on Charlie's shoulder and flashed a smile that made her knees weak. On his book jackets he always looked so stern.

"Colton, this is Ronnie Coleman. She works for Owen."

"Oh, sure. I heard all about you from Rita on my last trip to the post office."

"She brought us dinner. One of your favorites, honey," Alex said to her husband.

He grinned. "I heard. I love chicken pot pie."

Ronnie handed the casserole dish to Colton.

"Would you like to join us?" Alex asked. "We could have it for lunch rather than dinner."

"Yeah! You should eat with us."

She smiled at Charlie. "Thanks, but no, I have to get back to work. Owen had a crazy case come up at the last minute. Congratulations on the new baby. It was really nice to meet you both," she said to Charlie and Colton.

"You, too. Drive safe." Colton opened the door for her.

She walked to the car, still in a state of awe. She'd just met one of her favorite authors, and he was Alex's husband! Would it be too fangirl of her to bring her stack of books over to be signed? She'd have to ask Alex.

Suddenly the sun broke through the clouds, fracturing the funk she'd put herself in ever since discovering Kevin was Mystery Man.

After several more hours at work, Ronnie walked through the square toward Pages Bookstore. One more present for her dad and she'd have her Christmas shopping done. The temperatures weren't as frigid as they had been a week earlier, and most shops were still open, the lights around the windows looking so festive.

She stopped at the huge pine tree, the colorful lights shining bright in the night. She'd been moving into her new apartment during the tree lighting ceremony and Christmas parade, so she missed them. But next year she'd be sure to attend all the town's celebrations.

She turned when she heard footsteps. Kevin came toward her, the sound of his boots on the walkway echoing in the quiet. As he got closer, she could make out his serious expression. They hadn't talked since the night of the party. He hadn't tried to call or text since Monday when she broke their date. She still felt a little bitter that he'd taken away two friends in one day. She'd enjoyed exchanging texts with

Mystery Man, and she'd enjoyed Kevin's company even more.

He stopped in front of her. "Hi."

"Hello," she said, trying to sound nonchalant. She wouldn't allow him to see how hurt and betrayed she felt.

"I assume you put two and two together and know it was me who called the wrong number a few weeks ago."

"Yes." She studied him for a long moment as he watched her back. "I also put two and two together and realized you've been lying."

He shook his head, then wrinkled his nose in the cutest way. "I might have omitted the truth, but I didn't lie."

"But you knew. The day of the church bazaar, you knew."

"Not until after you left and I called."

"And hung up on me." She narrowed her eyes in an attempt to look menacing. "You knew when you met me at Noelle's. We were texting right before you showed up."

He took a step closer. "Yes, and we had a nice time."

"You knew when you came to the Christmas tree lot."

"Once again, we had a good time."

All that aside— "You still should have told me."

"Would telling you have made a difference?" he asked, holding his hands up in supplication.

She looked from him to the tree lights. A gentle snow had begun to fall, flakes landing on the branches. On her nose. She swiped the wet away. "I wouldn't be mad at you now."

"Why are you mad? Me not telling you the whole truth didn't change anything, did it? We got to know each other the same as we would have if you'd known. I didn't deceive you in any way other than I knew and you didn't. You're the only one who knows."

He took another step closer. "Sorry. That is a lie. I did tell my mom and stepdad after the bazaar. They encouraged me to get to know you through texts, but when I knew you were at Noelle's, I thought, why not get to know her in person? I wanted to see your pretty blue eyes, and your smile."

"You manipulated me just like my parents do. Do you have any idea how it feels to be made a fool? Do you have idea how it feels for a choice to be taken away from you?" She turned back to him, embarrassed that she'd sent the text to Mystery Man telling him she'd met someone.

"I'm sorry. I see now that I should have told you. Don't let my stupidity ruin something good. I didn't mean to hurt or embarrass you, Ronnie. I just wanted you to give us a chance, and I was afraid you wouldn't if you knew it was me texting." Kevin reached out and brushed a snowflake off her cheek. "I really like you, and I think you like me, so let's see where this goes."

He looked sincere. And he was right. She did like him. She'd made the choice to date him when she texted Mystery Man. He hadn't forced her to make that decision, though he would have known, which was an unfair advantage on his side. But what difference did that make in the end? Still, she wanted to know. "What did you do when I texted that I'd met someone?"

"Pumped a fist in the air."

She scoffed. "You did not."

"I did. Your text made me happy." Putting his nose to her temple, he inhaled like he was breathing in the scent of her skin. "*You* make me happy."

The simple act set her heart pounding. They certainly didn't experience love at first sight, but they had fallen into friendship pretty easily once she opened her eyes to the man he was. The times she'd spent with him had made her pretty happy too.

"Did you clean the snow off my car?"

"Am I in trouble for that too?"

"No, it was sweet. Thank you."

"You're welcome." He moved his nose to her neck, making her shiver, and not from the cold. "What do you say, Blue-eyes? Can you give us a try? See how we fit?" He'd wrapped his arms around her waist and pulled her closer.

She like his confidence, and the way he made her feel when he was close. "Would you have told me the truth if I hadn't found out?"

"Yes, I would have. Eventually. But I'm glad we got to know each other first. And I'm glad we got to know each other the way we did. How many couples do you know started out with a wrong number?"

"Don't toot your horn too loudly. I'm sure it happens."

He smiled. "What do you say. Can you forgive me?"

She wrapped her arms around his waist. "Maybe for a piece of mixed berry pie à la mode."

"That can be arranged," he said, settling her against him.

"Are you going to kiss my anytime soon?"

He glanced up. "No mistletoe."

"No, but there is snow."

"True. There is that." And he kissed her.

If you enjoyed *Snow and Mistletoe in Eden Falls*, I hope you'll continue reading! The next book in the Eden Falls Series is *Rumors in Eden Falls*

To keep up to date on new releases join my newsletter at TinaNewcomb.com.

Following is an excerpt from *Rumors in Eden Falls*.

CHAPTER ONE

"We've been dating for five weeks and I've never met your parents."

Leo Sawyer watched Gayle pull a string of gum out of her mouth, then twirl her finger around, collecting the line before sucking it off with a "pop" of her lips, like she was eight instead of twenty-eight.

Just one of her many habits she thought adorable and he found irritating.

"I've told you about my parents. They're usually so stoned they wouldn't remember meeting you, much less remember your name."

"Has Phoebe met them?"

They'd already discussed this on more than one occasion. "Yes, because I've known Phoebe forever."

"Do they remember her name?"

"Yes." *On a good day.*

She stretched out another strand of gum.

"Can you not do that in a restaurant?"

"This is a café." She glanced around. "Besides, no one cares."

I do.

"If I made you choose between Phoebe and me, who would it be?"

Easy choice. "There's nothing—"

"Going on between Phoebe and me," Gayle finished for him, trying to mimic his voice. She leaned forward, resting her arms on the table, her brown hair falling like a dark curtain on both sides of her face. "Except you're always together. If you're not, you're on the phone or texting each other. Almost every one of your sentences mentions her."

"You're the one who's bringing her up tonight."

When he first met Gayle, he'd been attracted to her energy and youthful nature. Now—not so much.

Gayle chewed with her mouth open, her gum snapping loudly. "She spends the night at your house."

Yep, Gayle hadn't been happy when she unexpectedly showed up at his house last Saturday morning, and Phoebe answered the door in a pair of his sweatpants and an old San Francisco T-shirt. "She stays in the guest room."

"Right. Like I believe that."

Everyone in Eden Falls believed he and Phoebe Adams were more than just friends, so why not Gayle? He didn't bother to argue since he couldn't force her to believe him.

"I'm normally not the jealous type, but I'm jealous of her. She's pretty."

"You're pretty."

Gayle scoffed. "You're supposed to say I'm a step higher."

"A step higher?"

"Yeah, like, *she's pretty, but you're beautiful,*" she said, again, attempting to sound like him.

He smiled. "Okay. You're beautiful." Which she was, in her free-spirit, carefree way.

"It's not the same if I have to tell you what to say."

He searched for a graceful exit to their conversation. Him canceling their Wednesday night date might be the cause of Gayle's grumpy mood, but he'd already committed to help Phoebe's sister, Izzy, move some furniture when a problem with the rental truck forced her to change the date at the last minute.

The waitress stopped next to their table and picked up his empty plate. Gayle had barely touched her dinner, but pushed her plate toward the edge of the table, signaling she was finished. "Can I get you anything else?"

"Just the check." Leo pulled his wallet out of his pocket.

"Excuse me. I'd like a piece of apple pie," Gayle said. "With ice cream."

Their waitress glanced at him with lifted brow.

"Just one, thank you."

"You could have asked me," Gayle said after the waitress turned away.

"You're right, but since you didn't eat dinner, I assumed you wouldn't want dessert."

"Would you have asked Phoebe?"

He wouldn't have to ask. "Phoebe never turns down dessert."

"How does she stay so skinny?"

High metabolism. "She's a cop. She works out a lot."

His phone vibrated, but he didn't pull it out of his pocket. Gayle was already antsy enough about his relationship with his best friend. If it was Phoebe, he'd call her back after dinner.

"I hear your phone, Leo. Aren't you going to answer?"

"Whoever it is can leave a message."

Gayle stretched her long legs out, plopping her heels on the seat next to his. *Not in a restaurant* ran through his mind. Again.

"You already know who it is. You might as well answer."

The waitress delivered the pie, and Gayle pulled the wad of gum out of her mouth and stuck it on her knife.

Why save it? She carried multiple packs in her purse.

"You never answered my question. If you had to choose between Phoebe and me—"

"I shouldn't have to choose. Why are you making this an issue?"

"I don't like to share." She nibbled at a bite of pie.

Gayle was about to draw a line in the sand and wouldn't be happy when he stepped over. In a way, Phoebe saved him. For that reason, he would always choose her. Life took them in different directions after high school, but he found his way back. Phoebe was his anchor in any storm.

He didn't like talking about his childhood, but he decided to share a minimum to get his point across. "My parents disappeared a lot when I was a kid. They'd go for groceries and stay gone for days. Phoebe was always there for me. I'm close to her entire family."

"No one had a great childhood."

Phoebe and her sisters did. "I'm simply saying, if forced to choose, I'd pick the Adams family over everyone else."

Gayle took another tiny bite of pie. "Have you ever kissed her?"

A sweet memory—one he'd never forget—floated through his mind. "Once. When we were nine."

His cell chimed with a text.

Gayle rested an elbow on the table, head in hand. "Did you tell Phoebe we were on a date tonight?"

He and Phoebe talked several times today, so, "Yes."

"And she still interrupts."

"If it *is* her, she wouldn't call or text if she didn't have a good reason." Leo shifted on the bench, feeling a little antsy himself.

"Then you better read the text. Maybe it's an emergency."

He tugged his phone free.

Call me when you're alone.

K, he texted back, then pocketed his phone.

"Phoebe?"

"Yes."

"Important?"

Must be or she wouldn't have texted. "She didn't say."

Gayle pushed the bowl of dessert away, the equivalent of one normal bite gone. "Call her. I have to go home anyway." She stood, wound a winter scarf around her neck, and pulled on a knit hat.

He started to get up, but she put a hand on his shoulder to hold him in place. "It's been real, Leo, but I don't see this working for me. You should be honest with yourself and admit you're in love with your *best friend*," she said using air quotes around the last two words.

"I'm not. At least not in the way you're implying."

"Right. You keep telling yourself that." She grabbed her coat and left Noelle's Café.

From his seat at the window, he waited until Gayle crossed the street and climbed into her car before he reached over with a napkin and pried her gum off her knife so the waitress wouldn't have to. After Gayle drove past, he called Phoebe.

"Where are you?"

He could tell something was wrong by her tone of voice. "Noelle's. Where are you?"

"Henry's."

"What are you doing in Harrisville?" he asked.

"Long story. Can you come?"

"I'll be there in fifteen," he said, grabbing his coat at the same time. He dropped a few bills next to the register and waved to the waitress. "Thanks. Keep the change."

The drive from Eden Falls to Harrisville was a straight

shot once he turned onto the highway, and the roads were clear despite the falling snow. Fifteen minutes later, he exited, taking a bridge over the river, then turned right at a rundown strip mall. Henry's, a twenty-four-hour diner that excelled in greasy food, sat at the far end. Ever since high school, he and Phoebe met at Henry's after a breakup—whether for celebration or commiseration. It was their place.

When he pulled in, he spotted Phoebe through one of the plate glass windows. Beautiful, wicked-smart, funny, quick-witted, snarky—all words to describe his best friend. Vulnerable—not so much, yet, that's how she looked tonight sitting at their usual booth.

The first time he met her, some older kids were teasing him about his hippie parents and geeky, outdated clothes. She'd shoved through the gathering crowd with fists raised.

So, it wasn't surprising that she became a cop, defender of the weak—protecting those who needed someone in their corner. Phoebe was that person.

Once inside, he slipped onto the opposite bench of the booth. "Hey, gorgeous. Did you and Brad have a disagreement?"

Phoebe pushed her blonde hair over a shoulder, revealing red eyes. He could count on one hand the times he's seen Phoebe cry.

Leaning forward, elbows on the table, he reached for her hands. "Phoebs, what's wrong?"

"Brad broke up with me."

He could count on one finger—now two—the number of times a guy broke up with her instead of the other way around. "Did he say why?"

"He doesn't believe you and I are only friends. He said I depend on your opinion too much."

Leo chuckled. "Did you tell him you never listen to me?"

She smiled, but it didn't quite reach her pretty brown

eyes, which cracked his heart. He hated to see Phoebe hurting.

"Were you serious about the guy, Phoebs?"

"We've been dating for three months."

"That's not what I asked. Do you love Brad?"

"No," she said, a look of guilt sliding across her face.

What's this about? Phoebe had only been heartbroken over a guy once. She usually dated for two or three months, then broke things off when the guy started getting serious. She and Leo shared the same attitude about marriage and children. Neither wanted to travel down that road.

Strangers would likely think they were witnessing a romantic moment if they saw him holding her hands. Slipping into a romantic relationship with Phoebe would be like wrapping himself in a warm blanket on a cold night because he already loved her more than anyone else in the world. But then he'd lose his best friend, and that would be like losing a limb.

He worried that one day a man would come along and sweep Phoebe off her feet, and he'd have to back away so she wouldn't be forced to choose—because she might not choose him. Every once in a while, that thought caused him a sleepless night.

"Look at it this way. You don't have to be embarrassed by his annoying habit of picking his teeth in public anymore."

"True."

"And no more stinky feet."

She wrinkled her nose like a bunny, a habit carried over from childhood. "I shouldn't have told you that." Her eyes misted over.

"What's with the tears?" He moved to the other side of the booth and wrapped his arm around her shoulders. "This isn't like you."

She swiped a napkin under both eyes. "I don't know what's wrong with me tonight."

"Is work going okay?"

"Yes. It's not work. I'm..."

"Flabbergasted because you're the one who usually does the breaking up?"

Phoebe snorted—a habit that seemed to run rampant among the five Adams' sisters. "No. Well, yes, but that's not it."

The tired waitress shuffled to their table. "You two want the usual?"

"Yes, please," Phoebe said.

"Add onion rings to my order, Esther," Leo added.

"You want blueberry pancakes with onion rings and a chocolate shake," Esther said rather than asked.

Phoebe held up two fingers. "Make that two orders of onion rings, and can I have some peanut butter on the side?"

"You two are weird," Esther muttered, then shuffled off to the kitchen.

Leo leaned forward so he could look into Phoebe's eyes. "What? You're going to order your own onion rings rather than eat all of mine?"

"Shut up and tell me about your date with Gayle."

He lifted a shoulder. "We broke up too. Gayle also doesn't believe you and I are just friends."

"Maybe we should line her and Brad up."

"Maybe." *His stinky feet and her disgusting gum habits might be the perfect match.* He tucked Phoebe's hair behind her ear so he could see her face.

She looked at him, her brown eyes intense. "Want me to talk to her? I can try to convince her you're not my type."

There was another problem with Gayle. Leo's one-eyed dog creeped her out. He might be able to overlook her gum-smacking, bubble-popping habit, but her not liking his dog was a deal-breaker. "It probably wouldn't have worked out in the end anyway."

"Because of Willy?"

"How can you not love a sweet dog with only one eye? Shouldn't that endear him to her even more?"

Phoebe picked up a packet of sugar. "I like Willy. Though, to be honest, it did take a little time to warm up to him. Not because of the one-eye thing. More the shedding all over my clothes thing."

Leo leaned back on the bench seat. "I'm done with women for a while."

Phoebe scoffed. "That will require a cell with bars."

"I see you haven't lost your sense of humor."

Esther delivered their chocolate shakes and Phoebe's side of peanut butter. "Pancakes and onion rings will be up in a minute."

"Thanks, Esther," Leo said.

Phoebe dipped her spoon in the peanut butter, then scooped up a bit of chocolate shake. "Sorry about Gayle. Despite her gum habit, I kinda liked her."

"Yeah, well, you might change your mind when I tell you she said I needed to choose."

"Wouldn't be the first time a girlfriend told you to do that. Remember Rachel?"

"How could I forget?" Rachel was his only serious girlfriend in high school. And to say she hated Phoebe would be an understatement.

"Sorry about that one, too. I know you liked Rachel."

"Not after she insisted I choose between you and her. It didn't help that I called her 'Phoebe' more than once."

She cuffed him on the chest, the exact reaction he'd expected. "Dork."

"At least I didn't do it during a make-out session like you did with Billy what's-his-face."

"Yeah, that was pretty bad," she said with a laugh.

"Bad?" Leo nudged her. "I got a black eye from your little mistake."

"You need to let that incident go, Leo. We were freshmen."

Esther delivered their pancakes, and Leo moved to the other side of the booth. "Billy wasn't. He was a junior and on the wrestling team."

"Sorry you got a black eye." She picked up her fork. "Hey, didn't you just eat dinner at Noelle's?"

"That was just an appetizer," he said, taking a huge bite. Nothing like pancakes to soothe the ache of a breakup. Only when he was halfway through his stack did he realize Phoebe wasn't stealing bites off his plate. Instead, she was staring at something over his shoulder. He glanced behind him to see what caught her attention.

An agitated man in his early twenties sat kitty-corner from them. His knee bounced nervously as he picked at a plate of fries and eyed everyone in the diner—a total of seven people including the cook and Esther.

When Esther went to the register with someone's check, the guy jumped up and pulled a gun.

"Give me the cash, lady," he hollered, his hoarse voice echoing around the small space.

Phoebe bolted out of her seat in an instant. When Leo started to get up, she put a hand on his shoulder. "Stay there."

She approached the man and he pivoted, pointing the gun at her chest. "Don't move!"

Leo's heart dropped to his stomach. Easing his phone from the table to the bench, he punched in 911, then silenced the volume so the guy with the gun wouldn't overhear the dispatcher.

Phoebe raised her hands in surrender. "Hey, I'm all for

robbing the rich. I just need to use the restroom. It's on the other side of you." She took a step forward.

"I said don't move." His shaking hand terrified Leo. The gun might go off accidentally.

His first instinct was to dive at Phoebe and knock her to the floor, but would the guy get a shot off before he could cover her?

"Mister, look, I really need to use the restroom. My onion rings are about to make a reappearance. If I can just slide past you so everyone here doesn't have to watch me puke, that would be great." She looked at Esther. "Tell Frank he should check the ingredients before adding rat poison to the batter."

As soon as the man's attention turned to Esther, Phoebe closed the distance in a flash. Sweeping out a hand and the opposite foot, she knocked both the gun and the guy to the floor. Then she pounced, agile as a cat, kicking the gun out of reach before flipping the guy facedown and pinning him to the floor.

Before Leo could react, Esther's eyes fluttered, and she dropped to the floor in a heap.

"Check Esther," Phoebe said.

To Leo's relief, a lone siren wailing in the distance grew louder, setting him in motion. He ran around the counter.

The guy struggled, but Phoebe held him tight. "Is she okay?"

"I think so. She's breathing." Leo patted Esther's soft, wrinkled cheek. "Wake up, Esther. It's over."

Leo didn't blame the older woman. His stomach was spinning at a sickening speed, and sweat beaded along his hairline. Sure, he'd seen Phoebe in action many times over the years. She could take down a guy twice her size in a heartbeat, but he'd never seen anyone point a gun at her heart.

"You okay?" she asked.

Anger bubbled up from a place he rarely visited. "No, I'm not okay. You could have been killed. What you did was reckless and irresponsible, and just like that stupid movie we watched last weekend. What were you thinking? He pointed a gun at your chest, Phoebs!" He swallowed when his voice cracked.

She had the audacity to grin.

The next thirty minutes were a blur of activity while two of Harrisville's finest rushed in, revived Ester, and hauled the would-be thief away. While Phoebe answered questions, Leo sat at their booth, rattling like a dried-up leaf skittering down a sidewalk.

Phoebe set a cup of coffee in front of him and sat down, leaning her head on his shoulder. "I was doing my job, Leo."

He wrapped his hands around the warmth of the cup, trying to soak it into his shaking body. "Your job is in Eden Falls, not Harrisville."

"My job is anywhere I am. I took an oath to serve and protect, and I did what any police officer would have done. Besides, I was afraid he'd hurt Esther if I didn't act."

He turned to look at her. "What about you? You're not invincible, Phoebe. You think you are, but you're not."

She smirked. "I was tonight."

"No, you were lucky tonight."

Minutes later, Leo got in his truck and followed Phoebe back to Eden Falls. When she turned off for Town Square and her apartment, he tapped his horn in farewell and headed up the mountain toward home.

Willy met him at the door with his usual happy greeting. Leo needed his dog's unconditional love and friendship more than ever tonight. He sat on the kitchen floor and let Willy pretend he wasn't a sixty-pound dog and too big to climb into Leo's lap.

When he'd found Willy wandering around on his parents' farm, the mangy animal looked like he could use a good meal and a friend. The dog shadowed Leo at a safe distance while he did a few odd jobs around the place to help his dad out. Once he finished for the day, Leo opened his truck door to leave and spotted Willy sitting near the front bumper, shaking like a leaf. Although Leo had never thought of having a pet, all it took was a quick gesture from him, and the dog jumped into the cab. That's how he became a pet owner.

Phoebe and her sister Stella named him after the pirate, One-eyed Willy, from the movie *Goonies*.

Leo finally disengaged, poured dry food into Willy's bowl, and left the dog wolfing down his dinner while he went to stand in front of the wall of windows that overlooked the small town of Eden Falls, Washington. The lights were blurred by the falling snow, but it looked picturesque in the distance.

Soon Willy came to stand beside him, his tail wagging so hard it slapped against Leo's leg. He patted his dog's head. "Hey, boy. Phoebs and I—and I use the word 'I' lightly—saw a little action tonight. She jumped in, and I froze."

He couldn't imagine what life would be like without Phoebe. She was his lifeline, his sunshine on a cloudy day, his salvation from parents who were so doped up most of the time they couldn't pronounce his name, let alone remember they had a son.

All his childhood memories involved Phoebe and her family. Her four sisters considered him a surrogate brother, and he loved filling that role. Her dad, Neil, called him "son" as often as "Leo." And Phoebe's mom, Beverly, had made a place for him in their home. He wouldn't have survived without the Adams family. He would have grown up in foster care, probably in another town, without Phoebe and her parents.

How would Sunday family dinners feel without Phoebe at the table? Would they continue the tradition? The thought made him sick to his stomach.

He flipped on the gas fireplace and sat on one of two butter-soft leather sofas. Willy jumped up and rested his head on Leo's thigh.

Gayle's *Have you ever kissed her* question stirred a memory from childhood.

It had been a sunny spring day, with birds singing and a breeze ruffling through the leaves. He and Phoebe were sitting side by side in one of his favorite hideout spots next to the river when he told her his plans to kiss a girl for the first time.

"Who?"

A golden-haired angel and the most popular girl in the fifth grade. "April."

Phoebe wrinkled her nose bunny-style. "She thinks she's so hot."

"'Cuz she is."

Phoebe flipped her long, blonde braid over her shoulder. "Well, I'm meeting Scott behind the school after my soccer game tomorrow."

Leo gritted his teeth in annoyance. Phoebe was always competing with him. Trying to be the first at everything. "Are you going to kiss him?"

"I'm thinking about it," she said, her tone as defiant as a nine-year-old could manage.

"You're only saying that because I'm going to kiss April."

"Am not."

"Are too."

"Well, so what? You're not the only person who can kiss."

He turned to her and crisscrossed his legs. "Do you even

know how? I mean, besides kissing your grandma or something like that."

"I know how as good as you do, Leo Sawyer."

A sudden thought interrupted his mad. "Do you think we should practice first? Like on each other? Then we'll know what we're doing with April and Scott."

Phoebe raised her eyebrows, and her cheeks turned pink. "You mean…kiss?"

"Well, yeah. I can tell you if you're doing it wrong before Scott does."

"And I can tell you before April laughs her head off."

"Hey!"

Phoebe glanced around, but they'd picked this spot because no one ever came down this way. They'd been fishing and sharing secrets here since they were little. She turned to him and crisscrossed her legs, so close their knees touched. "How do we start?"

"I guess we just touch our lips together."

Leaning forward, she gave him a quick peck but jerked back when their noses bumped.

"Ouch," he said, his eyes watering. "Turn your head."

She giggled and rubbed her nose. "Are you going to tell April to turn her head?"

"If we bump noses, I am. And you're supposed to close your eyes," he ground out. Leo hated that he didn't know what he was doing. By the fourth grade, a guy should know certain things, and this was probably one of them. His parents never told him anything. He always ended up learning on his own or asking Phoebe, but there were certain things a guy couldn't ask a girl.

"You're not supposed to say things like that either. In the movies, the man and lady just move their heads around. And you only know my eyes were open because yours were."

"I don't watch kissing movies. Let's just try again."

"Wait." She tugged lip balm out of her pocket and applied a generous amount. "Your lips are dry."

"Are they supposed to be greased up?"

"Makes sense. If you're moving your lips around and twisting your heads, they'll slide easier," Phoebe said, holding out the lip balm.

Leo greased up and handed the tube back. "Hey, it tastes like oranges," he said, licking his lips. He liked oranges.

"Don't lick it all off," she ground out. "I don't have that much left."

"I just tasted it. Geez, I'll buy you another one." With what, he didn't know. Most of the time Phoebe's mom or dad gave him money for school lunch because his parents forgot. He couldn't count on his parents to buy groceries so he could make a sandwich.

She blew out a breath. "Should we count to three?"

"Do they count to three in kissing movies?"

A frown creased Phoebe's brow again. "No, they just look into each other's eyes, then they kiss."

Leo leaned forward, elbows on knees, and Phoebe did the same. He stared into her brown eyes. He'd always thought her eyes were pretty, like a gorilla he saw at the zoo on a field trip in the third grade. "Is this long enough?"

"I guess. You have dirt on your nose."

He smirked. "Good thing you're not kissing my nose."

"Well, don't rub it on me."

Enough with the talking. Leo leaned forward and pressed his lips to hers. She smelled like oranges. The lip balm made his lips tingle.

She snickered. "How long do we stay like this?"

Leo pulled back and shrugged. "Jake said you're supposed to touch tongues."

"Gross! How does he know?"

"He said he kissed Natalie last week, and they touched tongues."

"Well, I'm not touching tongues with Scott. That's too gross. And my dad would get mad if he found out."

"Will he get mad if he finds out that we're kissing?" He really liked Phoebe's dad and didn't want to make Neil mad.

Phoebe lifted a shoulder.

"Let's just try it. I don't want to mess up when I kiss April."

Phoebe wrinkled her nose again. "Okay, but don't tell anyone, or I'll punch you."

"Like I want to tell anyone I kissed my best friend. You're like a guy."

"Hey, I can say the same thing about you being a girl!"

"Just hold still." He wrapped his hands around her upper arms and touched his lips to hers. "Open your lips, Phoebs," he mumbled against her mouth. When she did, he slipped his tongue between her teeth. His heartbeat kicked so hard he immediately leaned back and stared at her. Was he having a heart attack? That's how his grandma died.

"What are you looking at?" Phoebe asked.

"You're doing it wrong," he blurted, the only thing he could think to say.

"How do you know?"

"Your tongue isn't supposed to be all stiff."

"Yeah, well, you're supposed to brush your teeth. Go practice with somebody else." She jumped to her feet and stomped away.

After that day, they went their separate ways to master the more refined art of kissing.

ACKNOWLEDGMENTS

As always, I have to thank my amazing editor, Faith Free-woman at Demon for Details. She is kind and caring and brutal with a red pen. I appreciate her ability to correct my mistakes while safeguarding my voice.

Thanks goes to Jane Haertel of Crazy Diamond Editorial for polishing my manuscript so quickly. Her comments are always right on target.

I want to thank Dar Albert of Wicked Smart Designs, who is amazing to work with. She sees my vision even clearer than I do.

Again, beta reader, Jeanine Hopping, helped with a very early draft of this book. Her feedback is always appreciated.

I want to thank Stefan Newcomb for keeping my website updated.

And to all my family, a special thank you for your love, encouragement, and support.

Happy Holidays!

Tina

ALSO BY TINA NEWCOMB

The Eden Falls Series

Finding Eden

Beyond Eden

A Taste of Eden

The Angel of Eden Falls

Touches of Eden

Stars Over Eden Falls

Fortunes for Eden

Snow and Mistletoe in Eden Falls

Rumors in Eden Falls

Second Chance Romance Collection

When You Love Someone

Endless Love

Rhythm of Love

Second Chance Romance Collection

ABOUT THE AUTHOR

Tina Newcomb writes clean, contemporary romance. Her heartwarming stories take place in quaint small towns, with quirky townsfolk, and friendships that last a lifetime.

She acquired her love of reading from her librarian mother, who always had a stack of books close at hand, and her father who visited a local bookstore every weekend.

Tina Newcomb lives in colorful Colorado. When not lost in her writing, she can be found in the garden, traveling with her (amateur) chef husband, or spending time with family and friends.

Follow Tina on:

facebook.com/TinaNewcombAuthor

instagram.com/tinanewcombauthor

bookbub.com/authors/tina-newcomb

goodreads.com/tinanewcomb

pinterest.com/tinanewcomb

www.ingramcontent.com/pod-product-compliance
Lightning Source LLC
Chambersburg PA
CBHW030643190726
48286CB00008B/2629